THE BUDDING TREE

Originally published in Japanese as *Koiwasuregusa* by Bungei Shunju, Tokyo

Copyright © Aiko Kitahara, 1993

Translation copyright © Ian MacDonald, 2008

First English translation, 2008

Library of Congress Cataloging-in-Publication Data

Kitahara, Aiko, 1938-
[Koiwasuregusa. English]
The budding tree : six stories of love in Edo / Aiko Kitahara ;
translated by Ian MacDonald.
p. cm.
"Originally published in Japanese as Koiwasuregusa by Bungei Shunju,
Tokyo"--T.p. verso.
ISBN-13: 978-1-56478-489-6 (alk. paper)
ISBN-10: 1-56478-489-4 (alk. paper)
I. MacDonald, Ian. II. Title.
PL855.I6747K6513 2007
895.6'35--dc22
                              2007026628

This book has been selected by the Japanese Literature Publishing Project (JLPP),
which is run by the Japanese Literature Publishing and Promotion Center (J-Lit Center)
on behalf of the Agency for Cultural Affairs of Japan.

Partially funded by grants from the National Endowment for the Art, a federal agency, the
Illinois Arts Council, a state agency, and by the University of Illinois, Urbana-Champaign

www.dalkeyarchive.com

Printed on permanent/durable acid-free, recycled paper and bound in the
United States of America

THE BUDDING TREE

SIX STORIES OF LOVE IN EDO

AIKO KITAHARA

TRANSLATED BY IAN MACDONALD

Dalkey Archive Press
Champaign • London

CONTENTS

THE BUDDING TREE

I

LOVE'S CHILL WIND

The students who had just begun school the previous year were reciting their multiplication tables. Beside them the third-year pupils were leafing through their practice ledgers and entering figures on abacuses. During the morning's lesson they had practiced writing Chinese characters and numerals, copying out dates and shop names, like so:

> October 1—Edoya
> October 2—Shinagawaya
> October 3—Kawasakiya

Below each they had entered the value of goods sold on credit. Once they had finished their calculations, they wrote the total at the bottom and exchanged ledgers with the student sitting next to them. They had been instructed to make believe that they were a rice wholesaler or, in the case of the girls, his wife. They all seemed to enjoy the game—even the girls.

When the bell sounded at two o'clock, Hagino—who was teaching addition to the new children that had entered her school just that spring—looked around the classroom. Classes commenced at eight in the morning and ended at two in the afternoon. The children sat watching her with their hands resting on their knees.

"That will be all for today."

"Thank you!" they replied in unison, bowing politely before standing up and moving the desks to the side of the room.

The pupil in charge of calling roll that day went to a corner of the room and opened the attendance book. One by one, the students' names were called out and checked off, and the children were dismissed. After each child's name was called, he or she approached Hagino and said goodbye before leaving.

There were only eight boys and girls in the third-year class, but nineteen in the second year and twenty-four in the newest batch. In addition, two parents had recently come to see Hagino, requesting that their children be admitted to her school in the fall. One family had just moved to Hagino's Horiechô neighborhood, but the other lived clear on the other side of the Isechô moat in Honfunechô. The child's parents had heard of Hagino's reputation and preferred their son commute to her school rather than attend the one nearest them.

As she saw the children off, Hagino was feeling rather proud of herself. Six years before, when she had taken over the school following the death of her father, Yamanaka Tatewaki, students had left in droves. Enrollment had dropped from nearly seventy to just twenty-seven or twenty-eight. Parents began sending their children to other schools in Honfunechô or Horidomechô, believing that a female schoolteacher would be too lenient on her students. The spacious twenty-mat classroom had felt practically empty, with just a small group of children huddled in the middle.

It wasn't that female schoolteachers didn't exist in Edo—they did. But general opinion held them to be inferior to men. Even other teachers frowned upon them, citing the example of one teacher in Ôdenmachô who was prone to get emotional and scream at her students. But Hagino wasn't about to close her school just because female schoolteachers had a bad reputation. Even if she were left with only one pupil, it was her duty to make sure that the child learned to read, write, and use an abacus in order to smooth his path through life and spare him from social ridicule.

So, as her pupils dwindled in number year by year, she bit her lip and soldiered on, teaching the ones that remained how to enter sums in their practice ledgers. She taught them how to add and subtract so they could calculate what their profit would be if they bought a barrel of sweet saké for six *mon* and a sack of candy for three, then sold them for eight *mon* and four *mon,* respectively.

Then, the previous year, enrollment had begun to increase. Children in Edo generally left school after three years and went on to begin apprenticeships. Word had been getting around that Hagino's former students were all performing superbly in their new positions, without any need for additional training . . . Suddenly Hagino realized that the pupil who had called roll was saying goodbye to her. Once he had left the room and Hagino had heard the lattice door sliding shut after him, she went out into the front hall.

There was an area of dirt floor inside the front door where the children removed their sandals, and shelves on either side for storing them away that were now all empty. She checked that none of the children had forgotten anything. As she turned away from the door, she heard the voices of several children who were loitering in the street outside before heading home. Then came the sound of the front door being slid open with trepidation.

A smile on her face, Hagino turned around expecting to see one of the children returning to collect something. Instead there was a man standing just beyond the threshold—a well-built man whose appearance was nevertheless unprepossessing due to his small stature. He bowed to Hagino. She was just about to ask who he was but stopped herself, knelt on the wooden floor, and returned his bow. She had recognized his round childlike face.

Between the third and fourth blocks of Horiechô there was a street lined with shops selling wooden clogs, leather-soled sandals, umbrellas, and all manner of objects related in one way or another to the weather. For that reason, the street was known as Terifurichô, or "Rain or Shine Street." The man's name was Eijirô and he was an employee of the Tokiwaya, an umbrella shop.

"Can I help you?"

"Well, um . . ." Eijirô hesitated, looking away as Hagino, hands still on the floor, raised her face and made eye contact.

The poor man was sweating profusely, probably from walking around in the heat of the day. Hagino watched as large beads of sweat rolled down his forehead. She looked away. Realizing he was sweating, Eijirô hurriedly took out a handkerchief and wiped his face, then around his neck, and then his face again. Growing impatient, Hagino repeated her inquiry just as Eijirô was timidly opening his mouth to speak.

"Well, um—"

"Did you come to see me?"

"Actually, I would . . . um . . ." Eijirô looked at Hagino, his face betraying some inner turmoil. "I would . . . like to become a student here."

"What?" Hagino looked at him in astonishment.

She had no idea what age he could be. Twenty-four or -five perhaps? Did a man of that age really intend to study reading, writing, and arithmetic alongside seven- and eight-year-olds? she asked.

"No, I'm already familiar with the basics of letter-writing and bookkeeping," Eijirô replied. "I'd just like to improve my handwriting."

"In that case, you should find yourself a calligraphy master."

Instructors like Hagino only taught the basics of writing—phonetic Japanese syllables and standard cursive Chinese characters. She did not teach students who wanted to become skilled calligraphers or to learn styles such as block script or flowing grass script.

But Eijirô shook his head. "Calligraphy teachers only accept students with proper handwriting, not chicken scrawl like mine—they wouldn't give me the time of day."

"It's all I can manage just to teach these children—"

"Please don't refuse. I *need* you to teach me—I'm tired of my boss and the head clerk saying they can't read my handwriting."

"But the kind of writing I teach is geared to children."

"That doesn't matter. Please . . ." Eijirô made a deep bow, lifting his face slightly to look at her. His big round eyes seemed on the verge of tears. "*Please* say you'll teach me. After all, the teacher in Honfunechô has a class of adults who come to him to study the *Four Books* and *Five Classics* after all the children have gone home."

"Yes, but he's a very learned Confucian scholar. I'm just the daughter of a ronin."

"But our head clerk says you've got better handwriting."

"I'm flattered by the compliment but—"

"Does the idea of teaching someone like me bother you?"

"That's not it!"

"Then please let me study with you!"

Without realizing it, Hagino, still on her knees, had been edging further and further away from the door. Now her hips bumped up against the step leading from the hallway into the classroom behind her.

"Well . . . but will your boss at the Tokiwaya let you take time off to come here?"

She imagined Eijirô would say that he proposed to come after the shop closed, in which case she intended to refuse on the grounds that evenings were inconvenient for her. But Eijirô's eyes burned with a feverish intensity as he swore to make time to come in the afternoon.

"Are you sure? You mustn't keep me waiting, you know!"

"I understand. I couldn't come every day, of course. I was thinking of six times a month, say, on the third and fourth, the thirteenth and fourteenth, and the twenty-third and twenty-fourth. Would three in the afternoon be convenient?"

Hagino wanted to reply that it wasn't. But Eijirô kneeled in the dirt inside the front door and bowed deeply, resting his hands on the edge of the raised floor of the hallway.

"Please! Just one hour . . . half an hour even. In winter when it's too cold to keep the classroom doors open, you can just write out some words for me to sit and copy on my own if you think people might gossip."

Under the circumstances, she could hardly refuse.

"Could we start on the third, then?" asked Eijirô.

"I suppose so," Hagino consented grudgingly. The instant the words were out of her mouth she regretted it.

Eijirô gave a sigh of relief. He looked at Hagino, who was still somewhat taken aback by his forwardness. When her eyes met his he suddenly reddened in embarrassment. He quickly bid her farewell and slipped out through the lattice door.

—⚬⚬—

It was rare for Hagino's landlord's agent, Tazaemon, to call on her. Tazaemon's two daughters had both studied under her father. The last time she'd seen him was about six years before when he'd come to announce that his younger daughter was to be married.

"Please don't put yourself to any trouble," Tazaemon said as he watched Hagino unwrapping a box of sweets sent by a student's grateful parents. "You've made such a name for yourself, Miss Yamanaka—some of it is even starting to rub off on me!"

"You're too kind," Hagino smiled awkwardly.

This was the same Tazaemon who, a year after her father's death, had sent a messenger round ordering her to vacate the premises. It had come as no surprise that he worried about her being able to continue paying the rent. Left with just twenty-seven students after her father's death, another twenty had departed that year saying they were to start apprenticeships, and the school had attracted only four new students.

Tazaemon was widely reputed to be stingy and coldhearted, but to see him here smacking his lips as he tucked into the sweets and slurped his tea, anyone would think he was just a kindly old grandfather.

"Now I hope you won't think this presumptuous of me . . ." Tazaemon paused, looking at Hagino with a big grin. "The fact is, I've been asked to act as a matchmaker."

"Huh?"

"Simply put, there's a man who's extremely taken with you, Miss Yamanaka."

"Oh."

Looking down at her lap, Hagino raised her hand to her forehead so that he could not see the expression on her face. Regardless of who the man might be, it was not disagreeable to hear that she had an admirer.

"There's just one thing—he's an older gentleman. Now, how old might you be, Miss Yamanaka?"

Hagino hesitated. "Twenty-seven," she replied with an embarrassed smile.

"The man in question is forty-five. He has a son who's twenty-one."

Hagino was quiet. An age difference of eighteen years didn't bother her so much as the thought that in a few years the man would have retired from whatever work it was that he did.

She had at last reached the point where her little school was grow-ing. In the past, when she'd had fewer students by the year, she'd had to dip into the meager savings that her father had left her in order to pay the rent. When those savings had run out, she'd staved off hunger for a while by eating tofu lees. Yet she had refused to close the school, and had continued to teach her few remaining students how to tally purchases of sweet saké and candy in their account ledgers.

"I understand how you must feel." Tazaemon appeared to have read her thoughts. "I told him right off: a teacher with her reputation won't want to close up her school just like that. But he was insistent—said he'd be willing to wait a year or two if necessary." Tazaemon looked at Hagino and grinned even more broadly. "Now, I don't mean to sound negative, but these days there are lots of teachers in Edo. It's only a matter of time before a really good one opens a school in Honfunechô or Isechô. On top of that, Miss Yamanaka, you're . . ."

Tazaemon left his sentence unfinished. She had no doubt, however, what he had intended to say: "On top of that, you're a woman." The implication was that if a good male teacher were to appear on the scene, families in Horiechô wouldn't hesitate to send their children to him.

"Now, your father resigned himself to commoner status after showing compassion for his sworn enemy, isn't that right?"

Hagino frowned at Tazaemon's mention of a subject she would have preferred to avoid. He was referring to the story of how her father, Tatewaki, had come to be a schoolteacher. Her grandfather, Yamanaka Hyôbu, had been a samurai in a small fief in the West Coun-try. One night, under cover of darkness he was cut down in cold blood by a fellow samurai with whom he'd quarreled. The man fled, and Hyôbu's only son, Tatewaki, had determined to track down his father's murderer. As luck would have it, he found the man several years later, holed up in a rundown shack close to death.

Tatewaki could not bring himself to exact vengeance on a sick man, even though the man begged him to do so. Instead he did his best to nurse the man back to health, imploring him to get well so he could challenge him to a fair fight. But soon the man died, expressing gratitude for Tatewaki's kindness. Overcome by the senselessness of the man's death and the utter meaninglessness of it all, Tatewaki had taken it upon himself to ensure that his father's killer received a proper funeral. Then he headed for Edo to become a schoolteacher. As he often said later, he wanted to teach children not to make enemies.

"Your father owed his excellent reputation to the fact that people knew he had put aside a grudge to care for his enemy," Tazaemon said. Hagino remained silent. "For a while, your father was drawing students away from that teacher in Honfunechô. It stands to reason—after all, who wouldn't prefer a man who'd shown kindness to his enemy over a simple Confucian scholar?"

"That's true . . ." Hagino croaked, managing to speak at last.

"Your reputation, on the other hand, is due to the fact you're a good teacher, Miss Yamanaka. But if word got around that that teacher in Honfunechô can teach more advanced material . . ."

He seemed to be implying that her students would again desert her and she'd be left destitute. As before, though, Tazaemon left his sentence unfinished. He began tapping his forehead pensively.

"That's where having a husband can be a real source of support. At any rate, the man in question is dead set on marrying you—asked me to do everything I could to convince you, if you'll forgive my importuning."

"No," Hagino said, again somewhat hoarsely, shaking her head.

"Well, think about it at your leisure. He's a paper merchant in Muromachi. His business is rock solid, so money's not a problem."

"But—"

"His son's a fine lad . . . listens to his father."

"I don't know anything about business."

"He's aware of that." Tazaemon again looked at her. "I don't want to scare you, Miss Yamanaka, but teaching children is fine for now. But when you get older and have to close your school, you'll be all alone."

"But . . ."

Hagino's reply died in the back of her throat. The thought of growing old alone was constantly on her mind. Since turning twenty-five, a year had come to seem so short. It felt like only yesterday she'd told herself she still had fifteen years to go until turning forty, yet now there were just thirteen. She had never relished the freedom of living alone. Whenever the school day ended and she saw one of her students go chasing down the street after his mother who just happened to be passing by, she felt not so much sadness as fear.

But she went on teaching, not admitting her true feelings even to herself. She told herself she wasn't the only single woman in the world. That teacher in Ôdenmachô, for example—the one who yelled at her students at the slightest provocation—was over thirty and still single. And the proprietress of that upscale restaurant in Asakusa, the Moegi, where Hagino had been taken the other day by the local doctor and his wife, was divorced. She recalled how the owner had jovially declared, "Suffering at the hands of a lover is one thing, but at the hands of a husband? Never again!"

Hagino, however, did not know what it was to suffer at the hands of a husband.

"Please take your time and think about it." Tazaemon slurped down the last bit of tea in his cup and stood up.

She accompanied Tazaemon to the entrance hall to see him off, trying to hide the fact that the conversation had left her feeling rather depressed.

"I'll be waiting for your reply. I think it's an offer well worth considering."

As he reached out to open the front door, it slid back on its own. Across the threshold stood Eijirô, who had raced over from Terifurichô.

Hagino remembered that today was the third of the month.

—◦◦◦—

"Miss Yamanaka . . ."

At the sound of Eijirô's timid voice, Hagino awoke from her reverie. She was seated at a low Chinese-style table in her large classroom. Facing her, about three feet away, sat Eijirô at a small writing desk. He was trying to indicate that he was eager for her to finish writing out the text for him to copy.

Hagino's brush had stopped in the middle of writing the words, "With humblest regards." Pinned down by a paperweight, the sheet of paper in front of her fluttered in the breeze blowing through the open shoji.

"Are you feeling all right, Miss Yamanaka?" Eijirô looked at her, blinking as though staring into a bright light.

"No," she replied curtly, resuming her writing.

It was annoying the way Eijirô's eyes always darted away from her whenever she looked at him, yet as soon as she averted her gaze she could feel them entwining themselves about her like a spider's web. Normally she would have simply put up with it. But Tazaemon's mention of her father had left her in a bad mood, and she found it more than a trifle annoying—downright irritating in fact—to have Eijirô staring at her in that strangely disconcerting way of his.

Hagino thrust the writing sample in front of Eijirô and turned to look out at the garden. The bush clover, which had been allowed to grow unchecked, had burst into a profusion of red flowers seemingly overnight.

Just like back then, she thought to herself.

The bush clover had been in bloom those many years before when she'd come running home after her last meeting with the man she once thought would become her husband. She'd been seventeen and her mother had recently passed away. "Why did she have to die?" she reproached her father with tears in her eyes.

Hagino thought about the man she'd been in love with, Minegishi Sôin. In retrospect, it was ironic that her father, Tatewaki, had provided the occasion for her first encounter with Sôin, a young up-and-coming nativist scholar. Sôin's own father, Minegishi Hansai, himself a famous scholar, had come to see Tatewaki after hearing of his reputation. Her father had felt deeply honored by the great scholar's visit and Hansai, for his part, had been impressed by the free and easy spirit that came through in Tatewaki's teaching—a spirit shared, he said, by the classical Japanese poets of the *Collection of Ten Thousand Leaves* and *Collection of Ancient and Modern Poems.*

It was inevitable that the two men should become close drinking companions. Hansai's son, Sôin, also started dropping by the school, and it was not long before he and Hagino developed an attraction for one another.

It had been in the fall of that year—the day after the moon-viewing festival, in fact, when the schoolchildren had gone house-to-house mischievously stealing the rice dumplings people had put out and stringing them together on bamboo sticks—that Hansai had come on his son's behalf to officially ask for Hagino's hand in marriage. Tatewaki received him not in the classroom but in the cramped living room piled high with desks and chests. Hansai asked that the wedding be held no later than the following spring. In May, he explained, his son would be setting out for northern Japan, where he'd been offered employment by a large fief. Sôin would be away from Edo for about three years.

Listening from the kitchen, Hagino had expected her father to be overjoyed and to call for her to break out the saké to celebrate. But no such call came. Listen as she might, she did not hear him so much as utter a word, much less give his consent. When, at Hansai's urging, Tatewaki did finally reply, she could hardly believe her ears.

"I refuse," he said in a low but firm voice.

"Refuse?" Hansai's voice was sharp.

Tatewaki explained he didn't want his daughter going so far away from home, but his friend was not to be dissuaded. Each accused the other of being selfish. The discussion turned into a heated argument that ended with Hansai storming out of the house.

Several days later, Hagino received a secret message from Sôin summoning her to his residence. The Minegishi estate was at that time located in Nihonbashi's Honchô district. When she arrived, she was shown into a spacious reception room where Sôin was waiting for her.

"There's something I wanted to tell you," he said. "I have not yet mentioned the matter to my father." Then he asked her, "What clan did Master Tatewaki serve before becoming a ronin?"

Hagino repeated the name she'd heard from her father.

Sôin frowned.

"Impossible."

"What?"

"No person by the name of Yamanaka Tatewaki ever served there."

There was more to it than that, continued Sôin. He had heard an interesting story from a man in Edo who worked for the fief in northern Japan where he had been offered employment. Apparently the official had got wind of Sôin's impending engagement to the daughter of someone named Yamanaka Tatewaki. It just so happened that the official had once had a distant relative by the same name. Moreover, this relative had also roamed the countryside looking for his father's murderer.

But *that* Yamanaka Tatewaki had passed away. He had turned up one day at his clan's storehouse in Osaka, a shadow of his former self. He was penniless, having exhausted the travel money given him by clan officials and his family having cut off his allowance. He was immediately given something to eat and tended to by a doctor, but in vain. He had died muttering despairing words at being unable to track down his father's murderer.

"When he arrived in Osaka, Tatewaki was so weak he could hardly walk," Sôin continued. "It appears he was accompanied by a ronin who was about twenty-five years old."

Hagino did not need to hear the rest to know what had happened. The ronin had been her father, who had been given a reward for helping Tatewaki. He had set out for Edo where, taking the name Yamanaka Tatewaki, he had told people he had once desperately tried to save his enemy's life, and had used the money to open a small school. The fictional Tatewaki's resolve to track down his father's murderer was a model of filial piety, and his equally strong determination to nurse his enemy back to health was a model of human kindness. Parents must have tripped over themselves rushing to enroll their children at the school of such a virtuous teacher. What Tatewaki taught his students above all else was to cultivate an easygoing spirit free of hate. It was no surprise that his fame grew and grew.

"I feel so humiliated!" Hagino had cried, shaking her father's knee and sobbing hysterically after fleeing Sôin's house with her hands over her ears.

"Forgive me." At a loss for words, her father had repeated the same phrase over and over. Hagino only shook her head. "Forgive me," he said again, prostrating himself on the tatami.

"Why did you carry on this disgraceful charade?"

"I hated my name," replied Tatewaki, his voice choked with emotion. "I hated the name my father had given me. He was expelled from his clan for stealing money."

"What is your real name, father?"

He paused before replying. "Igaya Jûzô."

Hagino stared at him in silence. It seemed her father had been replaced by a man she didn't know. "We could go into hiding," she suggested.

Her father shook his head. "I'm Yamanaka Tatewaki now."

"I know but . . ."

"I can't just go off and abandon the children. When it becomes known I'm really Igaya Jûzô and all my students are gone, then I'll go away."

Until then, he said, he was prepared to endure any amount of shame. At that moment, the look on his face belonged to the father she had always known.

From then on, she became his devoted assistant. He had been right: students came to his school wanting to be instructed by Yamanaka Tatewaki, and he had an obligation to see his job through to the end. If she and her father were to go into hiding, it wouldn't be long before everyone in Horiechô found out the truth.

When she was teaching, surrounded by her students, Hagino was able to forget all about Sôin. She found it adorable the way the children would bring their lunches from home just so they could eat with her, yet also unsettling that they listened to her more than their own mothers. She had no time to shed any tears over Sôin.

Two years passed, then three, and Hagino turned twenty. Rumors spread that she intended never to marry and to take over the school when her father retired. She did not mind, however. She had turned down several offers of marriage and had come to accept the fact that she would spend her entire life as a teacher.

But her resolve lasted only as long as her father was still alive. In the summer of her twenty-second year, Tatewaki passed away, uttering repeated apologies for having pretended to be someone else. Hagino suddenly felt lonely. In part this was because students had begun deserting the school, but what was worse was not having anyone to talk to.

If only I'd gotten married! She was besieged by pangs of regret. *What if I get old and can no longer teach?* The thought sent shivers down her spine.

Yet she was determined to keep the school open. Was she the only one who understood the joy of seeing an extremely withdrawn child—one who sat in a corner watching, never saying a word—quietly reach out and pick up one of the tiny seashells she used to teach numbers?

The idea of closing the school and getting married held no appeal. She longed to hear people say, "That Miss Yamanaka, she's her father's daughter all right." Still, whenever she received a marriage proposal such as the one communicated through Tazaemon, she couldn't help imagining herself when she turned forty—

"Miss Yamanaka?"

Eijirô's voice interrupted her reverie. It was nearly three in the afternoon. Outside the bush clover rustled in the wind. Inside the classroom, all was quiet.

Before taking a look at what Eijirô had written, Hagino dipped her brush in ink. Eijirô's calligraphy had a strange tendency to slope downwards to the right. Hagino had already scolded him about it, but bad habits were hard to break. She expected that today, too, she would have to correct just about every word he had written.

When she looked up, Eijirô's gaze was fixed on her.

Hagino looked away. Blinking, Eijirô cast his eyes downward.

***

Tazaemon's house was on the edge of Horiechô. It was a private residence, and standing outside it Hagino could hear the voices of his grandchildren. Beneath the eaves sat a pot planted with wild grasses presumably collected by one of the children.

Tazaemon appeared at the front door, a child clinging stubbornly to his neck. "You'll regret refusing an offer this good," he said several times as he sent the child back into the house. Then, muttering to himself, he added, "Puts me in an awkward spot, too."

Hagino could imagine Tazaemon, upon being asked by the paper merchant to act as a go-between, thumping his chest and saying to the man, "Don't worry, you're in good hands—leave everything to me!"

"I'm sorry—I'm best suited to being a teacher," she told him point-blank.

"Headstrong woman!" she thought she heard him say, clicking his tongue as she left.

Walking down one of Horiechô's side streets, Hagino ran into a well-built man who she recognized as the Tokiwaya's head clerk, accompanied by a shopboy. He greeted her politely, "Cold weather we've been having."

She replied cordially enough, but as she passed by she thought she saw a smirk appear on his face. For that matter, she couldn't remember the Tokiwaya's head clerk ever having greeted her so familiarly. Naturally, she said hello whenever she saw him. But since the owners of the Tokiwaya had no children, she was not so well acquainted with them or their employees as she was with her students' parents.

Suddenly it occurred to Hagino that Eijirô was the reason for the smirk on the clerk's face. The thought immediately dampened her mood. And if that were not enough, she was still annoyed about the way Eijirô had looked at her during his lesson.

I should have flatly refused.

I really should have.

Now that she thought about it, there was perhaps more to Eijirô's eagerness to take writing lessons from her than he was letting on. He was single, she was single—no wonder his coworkers' curiosity had been aroused. Everyone at the Tokiwaya from the shopboy up no doubt believed he was crazy about her. They were probably snickering about it behind his back, wondering what he saw in the twenty-seven-year-old unmarried schoolmarm.

It would not stop with the Tokiwaya, either. That shopboy would go blabbing to the other shopboys in the neighborhood about "our assistant clerk's girlfriend." They in turn would go and pass it on to the servants in their shops. Rumors of romance between Hagino and Eijirô were probably already spreading like wildfire.

What's more, Eijirô had worked at another umbrella shop until he turned seventeen. However, it had gone out of business, and he had had to use his connections to get a job at the Tokiwaya. In other words, he hadn't worked his way up in the shop as an apprentice. Such non-apprenticed employees were typically not entrusted with important tasks and it took them longer to get promoted. And it was impossible to start a family on anything less than a head clerk's salary. Hagino had heard stories about men like Eijirô who had changed employers in midstream and were still single at forty. They were known to drown their sorrows by carrying on with barmaids, dance teachers, and the like.

It wasn't unthinkable that people would connect such stories with the rumors about Hagino and Eijirô. If that happened, Hagino would get a reputation for being a loose woman. And if her reputation were tarnished, people would stop sending their children to her school. She would have to tell Eijirô that he could no longer take lessons from her.

Suddenly, an image of her large empty classroom after all the children had gone home flashed through her mind. She turned and looked back at the corner where the head clerk must have turned onto the main street. Then she set off once again at a brisk pace.

—⚬⚬—

"Miss Yamanaka! Miss Yamanaka!" A boy's voice was calling her from the garden.

Turning around, she saw the carpenter's son, Sadakichi, his upper body leaning against the veranda. He must have entered the garden through the back gate, apparently left open, that let onto the narrow alleyway separating her house from the one next door.

"What is it? If you've left something behind, you ought to come in the usual way, from the front."

"No," Sadakichi said, shaking his head, "I didn't forget anything. I . . ." His voice trailed off as he looked down at the floorboards. So there *had* been something troubling him after all—she'd noticed that he'd seemed strangely inattentive in class that day. "I did something bad."

Hagino invited him inside. Sadakichi clambered onto the veranda and entered the room. His eyes were bloodshot and filled with tears.

"Miss Yamanaka, I . . ."

"Yes?"

Sadakichi paused and took a breath. "I don't know what to do, Miss Yamanaka. I saw something last night—my mother and father . . ." He stopped, looking uncomfortable.

Hagino smiled. It was not the first time a child had confided this sort of thing to her. Her students were not all from families with shops on the main street. There were quite a few whose parents earned just enough to get by, working as wage laborers or street peddlers selling fish or repairing tobacco pipes, who nevertheless wanted their children to be able to read and write, and so they somehow managed to scrape together enough money to send them to school. Most of these children lived in tenements that had just one four-and-a-half-mat room. They slept alongside their parents and siblings, limbs atop one another, and if they happened to wake up in the middle of the night it wasn't unusual for them to see their parents in the act of making love.

Sadakichi's father was one such wage laborer, a carpenter by trade. The boy lived with his parents and his younger sister in a row of tenements behind a tofu shop. Hagino had often seen him being led by the hand to the bathhouse by his doting father, his sister Omitsu perched on the carpenter's broad shoulders. She could imagine the two together in the bath, his father telling jokes as he scrubbed Sadakichi's back. The shock of seeing his father in such a way that night must have left him speechless.

"Don't worry, Sada-chan. Listen, you have a baby sister, right?"

"Uh-huh."

"Well, Omitsu probably wants a baby sister, too. Your mother and father must be trying to make one for her." A strange look appeared on Sadakichi's face. Hagino wondered if what he had seen that night was flashing through his mind. "You'll have to understand these things if you want to grow up to be a good big brother. But for now, it would be best not to say anything to your father or your mother or Omitsu."

Sadakichi did not answer.

"Sadakichi? A good big brother wouldn't do that, right?"

Choking back tears, Sadakichi said he understood.

Hagino took out a box of sugar drops sent to her the day before by the parents of a student whose family ran a confectionary shop. Sadakichi, however, appeared in no mood to eat sweets. Having been told that he was now a big brother, he must be feeling as though adulthood had suddenly been thrust upon him.

"Have some, Sada-chan. Oh, and we mustn't forget to send some home for your sister."

Sadakichi ate a few of the sweets, apparently not quite sure what to make of them. Then, with his sister Omitsu's portion wrapped up in a piece of paper, he went off home. As he walked away she overheard

him say to himself, "Now I'm more grownup than Tome-chan!" referring to his playmate Tomekichi. For the moment he might feel more
mature than any of his friends, but that would probably be forgotten
as soon as he and Tomekichi were once again vying to see who was the
best at spinning a top or walking on stilts.

Hagino waited until the sound of Sadakichi's footsteps had reached
the end of the alleyway and faded into the distance. Then she went back
inside and dragged her desk into the middle of the empty classroom.
Eijirô would not be coming for his lesson that day. When he had come
nine days earlier, on the fourth, Hagino had informed him she was
unable to continue his lessons.

"Really?" was all Eijirô had said, his eyes cast downward.

She had been about to give in and say, "Well, just one more time
then . . ." But at that moment, Eijirô at last found the courage to look
up, and the reddish flush around his eyes and pug nose had told Hagino
all she needed to know about the inner turmoil he was holding in
check. *Good thing I refused,* she thought. She was glad, yet why did her
classroom feel so large and empty?

After Sadakichi had gone, Hagino tried to imagine the house the
boy was returning home to.

The front door would be wooden at the bottom with only paper
from the waist up. Inside, there would be an earthen floor and a cooking stove in the corner. In the adjoining small, four-and-a-half-mat tatami room, his mother would be mending her husband's torn clothes
while his sister, Omitsu, sat nearby folding the laundry. Omitsu would
squeal with delight at the sight of the sweets Sadakichi had brought
home. She would give one to her mother, who would accept it with a
pleased look on her face. Omitsu would trail after her older brother as
he took his stilts and headed out to play with his friends. When at last
the day drew to an end, Sadakichi's father would arrive home and take
his children to the bathhouse. Afterward, they'd sit down to a simple
dinner of rice, dried fish, and pickled vegetables, before turning in for
the night, huddled together practically on top of one another in their
tiny room.

Hagino envied them. Sadakichi and his family led a very comfort-
able life, in her estimation.

Just then, an image of Eijirô's heavy, downward-slanting writing flashed through her mind. Whenever she sat down beside him to correct this bad habit of his, his body went strangely rigid and he shied away from her, withdrawing to one side of the desk.

Hagino heard the sound of the front door being opened. She wondered if it was perhaps Eijirô, having forgotten that she had cancelled his lessons.

"Is anyone home?" The voice was muffled and indistinct—nothing like Eijirô's. At the same moment, the shoji leading into the classroom from the hallway slid open. A man with thinning hair stuck his face into the room.

Hagino frowned. She had never spoken to him before—not even to say hello—but she knew his name and occupation. He was Goroji, the local policeman.

"No need to make such a face. Just doin' my job, miss."

Hagino quickly got up and went over to the sliding door to forestall any attempt on his part to enter the classroom. But Goroji was simply sitting in the entrance hall waiting for her.

"Are you familiar with a man by the name of Gihei, Miss Yamanaka?" he asked her.

"No," she replied, firmly shaking her head.

Goroji folded his arms over his chest and looked at her. "That's odd," he responded. "Yesterday I caught a petty thief named Gihei—he claims he spent the money he stole to send his kid to your school."

"I think there must be some mistake," Hagino said with a lilt of her head. She hadn't accepted any new students lately, she told him, and none of her children's fathers were named Gihei.

A faint smile rose to Goroji's lips. "Well, that's 'cause he probably didn't use that name with you."

"In that case, what name did he use?"

Again Goroji smiled. "If I knew that I wouldn't have to go to all this trouble."

"But . . ."

"At any rate, he said he paid you the money," Goroji said, raising his voice. Hagino was cowed into silence. The policeman continued, "So you've still no idea, Miss Yamanaka?" The smile—gone a second earlier—returned to Goroji's face. "Once stolen money's been spent it causes all sorts of problems, you know."

Finally, it dawned on Hagino that Goroji was demanding a bribe.

When a thief was apprehended and confessed to a crime, it was customary for the recipient of the stolen money, as well as his land-lord and the neighborhood officials, to be called down to the City Magistrate's Office for questioning. This was inconvenient for the busi-ness owner but it was even more of a hassle for the landlord and local officials. Hence, the person who had unwittingly received the money was typically obligated to pay a small sum to his landlord to settle the matter and to treat all the concerned parties to a meal at some fancy restaurant. It didn't matter whether the thief had spent a large amount of money or only bought a handkerchief. Most people, upon being informed that they had received stolen money, would dutifully go round to their local policeman with a small bribe and ask him to "spare them the trouble of an investigation."

There were some unscrupulous policemen who, once they had gotten a taste for such graft, would look for easy targets to shake down whenever they needed a little extra cash and make up a story about stolen money. Goroji was such a policeman.

"Well, miss, I just came round to let you know what this Gihei told me."

Hagino stood up. Without a word, she went over to one corner of the classroom, took out a gold coin and wrapped it in a piece of tissue paper. She had once happened to overhear somewhere that the going rate for such bribes was one *bu*. She returned to the entrance hall and placed the money in front of Goroji.

The policeman's shoulders shook with laughter.

"I was hoping for a little more thanks than this!" He smiled. "You see, this Gihei mentioned a man by the name of Igaya Jûzô." A shiver ran down Hagino's spine. "If you don't know him, then that makes my job a whole lot easier. I'll just turn Gihei over to my boss down-town. But since I was in the neighborhood, I thought I'd check with you—it'd look bad if it turned out you knew him."

"Igaya Jûzô . . ." Hagino stumbled over the words. Her mouth felt dry. "What do you intend to do about him?"

"Don't worry. Gihei can give whatever statement he wants—it won't make any difference. You see, Igaya Jûzô is dead." A slight chuckle escaped Goroji's lips. "This Igaya Jûzô was a pitiful case. His father was an embezzler and he himself masqueraded as someone else—made up a story about avenging his father's murder."

"So what do you want me to do?"

"Ah, I see you're an intelligent woman. Just like a schoolteacher should be!" Goroji folded his arms and looked at Hagino as though he were sizing her up. Then he held up the palm of his hand.

"Five *ryô?*" Hagino asked.

"You must be joking—for overlooking this sort of deception? Try adding another zero."

"Fifty *ryô!* I couldn't possibly—"

"You don't have to pay right away. But if you keep me waiting too long, I might have to go talk to your landlord and tell him his tenant's been living under false pretenses!"

Goroji stood up, thrusting his hand into the breast of his kimono.

In addition to an entrance fee of one or two *shu,* Hagino charged her students three hundred *mon* in tuition, payable five times a year. In her working-class neighborhood, most of her students' parents were merchants of one kind or another, so she sometimes received deliveries of rice, miso and other commodities. Little by little, she'd been able to put some money aside.

But she only had fifteen *ryô* in cash at home. She knew that without even having to open her moneybox. In addition, she saved up money each month to buy sweets for the children on the twenty-fifth, the day sacred to Tenjin, the god of learning, but that only amounted to two or three *bu.*

Hagino covered her face with her hands. She had no choice but to borrow the money. The only person she could think of was Tazaemon. She hurriedly slipped into her sandals and dashed out of the house.

At first Tazaemon must have thought Hagino had come to say that she had changed her mind. His face was wreathed in smiles as he ushered her into his sitting room. His manner changed abruptly, however, once he had heard the reason she had come. The rumors about his stinginess, it seemed, were true.

Hagino left Tazaemon's house in short order.

The neighborhood was bathed in the evening glow. It must have been past four o'clock. Hagino had the impression that she had heard the tolling of the bell as Tazaemon was explaining why he didn't have even one spare *mon* to lend her.

She had fifteen *ryô* in her moneybox—fifteen *ryô*, two *bu*, and two *shu*, if she counted her savings for the children's monthly sweets. Where was she to find the remaining thirty-four-odd *ryô?*

She had one or two students whose parents had always said they would do whatever they could to help Hagino if she ever needed it. There was Tokumatsu's father, a clog maker, for example, and also Osen's parents, who owned a discount shop in Terifurichô. She could probably count on them to lend her two or three *ryô,* no questions asked. There were a dozen or so of her students' houses that she could go to bowing and scraping, borrowing a few *ryô* here and there, but it wouldn't be long before people would want to know what she needed the money for.

No, I can't borrow. I just can't.

But if she didn't, her father's deception would come to light.

Should she borrow the money? If she did, people would start asking questions and sooner or later the truth about her father would come to light. For that matter, could Goroji be counted on to keep his silence even if she paid him the money?

"Miss?" A man's voice was calling her. "Excuse me, Miss Yamanaka?"

Hagino stopped and turned around absent-mindedly. On the other side of the street, she saw the outline of a round childish face, turned in her direction.

"Eijirô . . ."

She instinctively took a few steps in his direction before averting her eyes, just as Eijirô always did upon entering her classroom. She had the strange sensation of bumping into an old friend—yet wasn't it only yesterday she had found the mere thought of his gaze annoying? Her own capriciousness confused her.

"Is something the matter?" he asked.

Hagino could feel his eyes staring at her.

"No." Hagino shook her head, still avoiding his gaze. She expected that would put an end to the conversation and Eijirô would turn and walk away. But with her eyes still on the ground, she became aware of him approaching her with tentative steps.

"You don't look at all well, Miss Yamanaka. I almost walked by without even recognizing you."

Perhaps it was the state of her nerves, but she felt about to burst into tears. Eijirô continued hesitantly, "If I'm not imposing, won't you tell me what's troubling you?" Hagino said nothing. "I'm nothing if not discreet."

Hagino looked up at Eijirô. He blinked several times and turned his face away.

"Goroji . . ." The name spilled out of her mouth before she knew it.

Eijirô glanced at her. He seemed to be urging her to say more. Encouraged somewhat, she told him what had happened.

There was no mistaking Eijirô's surprise. No matter how high she had ranked in his affections, it was inevitable the scales would fall from his eyes once he learned she was the daughter not of Yamanaka Tatewaki but of Igaya Jûzô.

"I'm sorry you had to listen to me talk about something so shameful. But please, for my father's sake, do not speak of this to anyone." Hagino bowed deeply.

"If you ask me," she heard Eijirô say quietly, "I don't think it's anything to be so ashamed of, Miss Yamanaka."

"Huh?" She looked at Eijirô.

Again he shifted his gaze. "It's not as though Master Tatewaki did anything terrible in taking someone else's name."

"But . . ."

"My real name is Sanjirô. Eijirô is the name they gave me when I was hired to work at the Tokiwaya. If I quit or become head clerk, then someone else will become 'Eijirô.' Isn't it sort of the same thing with your father?"

He glanced at Hagino and smiled. "Your father's luck changed when he became Yamanaka Tatewaki—he became a great man. What could you be more proud of? Thanks to him, the children who live around here learned how to read and write from as fine a teacher as ever lived."

Hagino stared at Eijirô without so much as blinking. *That's one way of looking at it,* she thought.

She pictured the faces of all the grateful parents she had seen over the years. The couple that peddled soba noodles on the streets until late at night who had told her with tears of gratitude that their son had gotten a job with a reputable firm. The carpenter and his wife who were overjoyed that their daughter was to take up service in a large emporium where she would be trained in proper etiquette. And there were many others. If only Eijirô had come into her life sooner! Then her father might have passed away knowing he had done the right thing in becoming Yamanaka Tatewaki.

But then she noticed the smile had vanished from Eijirô's face.

"I wanted to work under a different name, too," he said.

Puzzled, Hagino tilted her head to one side.

A different kind of smile spread across Eijirô's face. "The Tokiwa-ya's never had an 'Eijirô' who went on to become head clerk."

"Really?"

"As you know, I didn't start out as an apprentice there. I didn't want to get stuck with this unlucky name, but I had no say in the matter. Still, I wanted them to say I was the best 'Eijirô' they'd ever had. But my handwriting . . ."

Eijirô stopped short and Hagino responded with a deep bow. It occurred to her that the only reason both she and her father had worked so hard to be good teachers was to conceal his true identity.

Then she heard the diffident Eijirô say, "As for the matter of Goroji, would you mind leaving that to me?"

Had she heard him correctly? But Eijirô repeated the question.

"I'll go downtown to Hatchôbori—I know a police sergeant there and I can ask him to tell Goroji to leave you alone, Miss Yamanaka."

"I couldn't ask you—"

"Don't worry, I work in a shop."

An Edo merchant would take whatever steps necessary to protect his business, and having the law on his side was part of that. This meant regularly greasing the palms of the local police sergeants and inspectors, just in case their help was ever needed to avoid the trouble of an official investigation.

"At the Tokiwaya, I'm the one in charge of doing that." Then he added with a low chuckle, "They'll let me do that much—even if they won't trust me to place orders and negotiate with our suppliers."

When Eijirô had seen Hagino home, she asked him quietly, "Now about money . . . ?"

"Yes, I'm sorry but . . ." Eijirô blinked a few times and looked away, a pained expression on his face. "I wish I could say that won't be necessary but the fact is, I'm a bit short right now."

Hagino disappeared into the house and retrieved the contents of her moneybox and the stash she kept for sweets. She handed the money to Eijirô along with her coin purse.

Eijirô looked directly at Hagino for the first time. Now she was the first to look away. A smile rose to his lips which seemed to say, leave everything to me.

"This will be plenty," he said, taking only five *ryô*. "I'll return tonight without fail, although it might be rather late."

Eijirô blinked again and looked down at the ground. Closing the front door behind him, he lowered his head and set off at a brisk pace. To the casual observer, he looked simply to be a man with an unlucky name who had failed to move up in the world.

Hagino went back into her classroom and put the remaining money back in the box. After lighting a lamp and sitting down at her desk, she still felt restless. She knew Eijirô wouldn't return anytime soon and would come only after he'd finished work at the shop. Nevertheless, she got up again and again and went into the entrance hall thinking she'd heard the sound of his voice. From where she stood looking out through the lattice door at the back street, all the shadows that passed looked like Eijirô's, and she could not resist opening the door to have a look.

Time passed slowly. She waited so long for him to return that it felt as though time had stopped.

"Is anyone home?"

At last she heard his voice and the sound of the front door opening, and ran excitedly out of the classroom. Eijirô stood inside the front door holding a lantern, his sleeve partly obscuring the name of the Tokiwaya written on it. Wearing only tabi on her feet, Hagino stepped down onto the earthen floor.

"Everything went just fine," said Eijirô, speaking quickly as though anxious that someone in the street might overhear. "There's no need to worry. Anyway, it's late. I'll come back tomorrow and tell you all about it."

Hagino's words of thanks caught in her throat and remained unuttered.

"All right then." As Eijirô made to leave, Hagino gently grabbed his sleeve. She could see the Tokiwaya's name on the lantern. The light inside flickered.

Without a word, Eijirô started to pull his sleeve away. She shook her head, looking as though she were about to cry.

"Miss Yamanaka, I . . ."

She understood. She knew deep down in her heart that Eijirô had no ulterior motive in going to Hatchôbori on her behalf. She knew, and for that very reason his feelings touched her all the more.

Eijirô gently removed her hand from his sleeve. "Let's talk tomorrow."

Hagino stepped outside and watched as Eijirô's figure receded quickly down the street, almost as though he were fleeing. For a while, his diminutive shape was silhouetted against the darkness by the lantern dangling down by his feet, but in time that too faded, leaving only a small point of light in the starless night.

At that moment, Hagino thought she saw Eijirô turn and look back.

II

⮾ EIGHT-TENTHS A MAN ⮾

The throng along Nihonbashi Avenue comprised every form of humanity: men and women, young and old—from samurai and craftsmen to merchants' wives with their pretty daughters. It was a typical afternoon in Aburachô.

Just as Kanae had been about to leave the house, her landlord had dropped by and detained her, chatting at length about when the communal well was to be dredged. Now it looked as though she would be late for her appointment.

Another new year! she had thought to herself only yesterday—or so it seemed. And here it was already the end of April. Quickly threading her way through the crowds basking in the gentle spring sunshine, Kanae felt beads of perspiration beginning to stand out on her brow and chest.

At last she caught sight of the familiar square signpost bearing its trademark emblem of a crane with its wings outspread to form a circle. Above it were the words "Book Merchant." The sign belonged to the Tsuruya Senkakudô, the venerable Edo publisher specializing in illustrated books.

In her haste Kanae practically broke into a run. Stopping in the shade of the large signboard, she took out a handkerchief and dabbed the sweat from her forehead and neck. Having caught her breath, she was just about to go inside when Masukichi, the shopboy, came dashing out. Kanae called him.

"Ah, Miss Rikô."

Hasegawa Rikô was Kanae's professional name in her role as the Tsuruya's principal calligrapher. She copied out the drafts of books by popular *gesaku* writers before they were carved onto wooden blocks for printing.

Saying he would inform Kiemon, the Tsuruya's proprietor, that Kanae had arrived, Masukichi went back inside the shop and through to the back. Apparently Kiemon was with another visitor at the moment. The deputy head clerk straightened a sheaf of colored wood-block prints and called out to Kanae inviting her to wait inside. Kanae thanked him, stepped inside, and sat down on the tatami at the front of the shop.

From somewhere came the strains of a shakuhachi—probably an itinerant monk seeking alms, thought Kanae. Next to her, three girls laughed gaily as they browsed the actor portrait prints for sale. On the other side of them, a man who looked like he had just come into town from the countryside was buying a thick illustrated potboiler to take home as a gift.

"My, the writing in this one is easy to read!" he was saying. The clerk glanced in Kanae's direction and smiled. The calligraphy for the book the man was holding was Kanae's handiwork. She had copied out the text and a famous artist had done the pictures, and then the blocks for both text and pictures had been carved separately by craftsmen specializing in such work. Kanae suddenly had the urge to go up to the man and tell him that it was her handwriting he was admiring.

She hadn't always had taken such pride in her work. On the contrary, she had thought of quitting on numerous occasions. But now she saw the wisdom of something her friend Hagino, a school-teacher, had once told her: whenever she saw one of her formerly illiterate students learning to write difficult Chinese characters, she felt a tremendous sense of satisfaction that enabled her to forget all the nasty slurs about her being an old maid who was just trying to follow in her father's footsteps.

"Master Tanehiko's new book is finished," the head clerk said, addressing Kanae. Apparently her new commission was to copy Ryûtei Tanehiko's latest work. Yesterday the shopboy Masukichi had come to Kanae's house in Tadokorochô to tell her that Kiemon had finally persuaded Tanehiko to write another book for the Tsuruya.

Tanehiko was currently the most popular *gesaku* author in Edo. Since publishing the first volume of his novel *The Fake Murasaki and Rustic Genji* three years before in 1829, the Tsuruya's sales had shot up. And now Kiemon had just put out volumes six and seven. Tanehiko's popular series had single-handedly revived the bookseller's flagging fortunes, just as rival upstart publishers had been threatening to overtake the old established firm.

"Sorry to have kept you waiting, Miss Rikô," said Masukichi, trying his best to sound grown-up as he emerged from the back of the shop. Though the other visitor still hadn't left, Kiemon had instructed the shopboy to show Kanae through to the small room at the foot of the stairs.

Bowing politely to the head clerk, Kanae stood up and made her way through the shop. In the left corner a curtain dyed with the Tsuruya's white crane emblem hung halfway to the ground. Beyond it was a narrow corridor that led to a staircase. At the bottom of the stairs was the small room where the owner Kiemon often met with block carvers and printers.

Kanae supposed that Kiemon's other visitor was a carver. The new season at the Nakamuraza theater would begin in June. If the Tsuruya intended to release portrait prints of the actors in time for the opening, the blocks would have to be sent to the printer's very soon. And yet the voice she heard coming from inside the room held a note of desperation.

"You've been stringing me along like this for ages saying you don't know when you'll be able to publish it."

Kanae stopped in her tracks. The man must be a writer or artist who had come to urge Kiemon to hurry up and publish his work.

"How many times do I have to tell you?" Kiemon replied icily. "It's not so simple. Before we can move ahead with your book, the publishing guild officer has to make sure it bears no similarity to any existing work."

"Now just a minute! Are you saying I plagiarized someone else's work?"

"Nobody's accusing you of any such thing. This is routine procedure—it doesn't matter who the author is. The local headman will only give us permission to publish once the guild has checked your book thoroughly. You of all people should be aware of that."

"Yeah, right." The man spoke as though such things were no concern of his. "But listen, that two-bit publisher Hoeidô sent you my manuscript last New Year—over twelve months ago! Do you expect me to believe the guild is still looking into it?"

"Believe me, we're eager to have your work published as soon as possible."

"Is that so?" the man replied. "By the way, whatever happened to that landscape series of Hiroshige's? The one Hoeidô wanted to publish but was short on cash. I heard they were planning to come to you for help."

"Oh, yes—*The Fifty-Three Stages of the Tôkaidô*."

"That's the one. Word is that Hiroshige's landscapes are masterpieces. Kunisada and Kuniyoshi can't hold a candle to them."

"Perhaps, but that doesn't necessarily mean they'll be commercially successful."

"Then again, I suppose if you helped Hoeidô publish Hiroshige's series and it turned out to be a big hit, you'd have a new rival on your hands, wouldn't you? *The Fake Murasaki*'s been keeping the Tsuruya afloat, but all that could change."

"Come now, you give me too little credit. As a matter of fact, I went ahead and lent Hoeidô the money they needed. Hiroshige's pictures will be published next year."

"But then why—"

"Excuse me . . ." Kanae called out from the other side of the shoji. She had not intended to stand there eavesdropping, but her curiosity had got the better of her and she had hesitated a bit too long before making her presence known.

"Ah, Kanae, is that you? We've been waiting." Kiemon sounded relieved at the interruption.

Kanae put her hand on the latch and was about to open the shoji, but before she could do so it was flung open from inside.

"I must be leaving."

A tall man emerged from the room and bowed to her, then stalked off down the corridor before Kanae even had a chance to utter a word of greeting. She watched him go. There was something familiar about his appearance, from which she judged he was a ronin. Kanae quickly probed her memory. She recalled a day not long ago when she had gone to Ryûtei Tanehiko's house to offer the customary New Year's greetings. There had been a man there by the name of Iguchi Tôi, a disgraced former shogunal retainer who was now a *gesaku* writer. He had been almost too drunk to walk, much to the horror of Tanehiko's other disciples.

That was the man Kanae had just seen.

Kanae heard the sound of the front door being opened. Whoever the visitor was, he seemed to have stepped inside but did not announce himself. Her father had left a while ago saying he was heading over to Ryôgoku to see what was showing at the vaudeville theaters. It was too early for him to have returned home already.

Perhaps it's Masukichi, she thought. Yesterday, shortly after she had returned home from the Tsuruya with the latest installment of *The Fake Murasaki,* a messenger from Tanehiko himself had arrived asking her to hold off on copying it for the moment. Apparently he had made some major changes to the manuscript and would be sending a new version around to her the next day. She had been expecting it to arrive any minute.

Kanae had been in the middle of copying out a word puzzle. She put down her brush and stood up.

Her house was located down a back street. Beyond a pair of sliding doors to the right of where she was seated at her desk was the six-mat room that housed the family's Buddhist altar and served as her father's sitting room. On the other side of Kanae's three-mat room was a pair of shoji opening onto an entrance hallway with a wooden floor. The visitor appeared to have seated himself in the hallway—Kanae could see the faint shadow he cast on the paper doors.

In accordance with proper etiquette, Kanae kneeled on the tatami and slid open one of the shoji. The man turned and looked Kanae directly in the eye; a smile played at the corners of his mouth.

"Well, it's been a long time, hasn't it?" he said. "But that's as much my fault as it is yours, I suppose."

Kanae was speechless. The man seated on the step was none other than Ryônosuke, her former husband.

"You haven't changed a bit, Kanae."

Four years had passed since Ryônosuke had divorced her. "Nor you," she replied, almost in a whisper, turning her face away from him.

Ryônosuke chuckled hoarsely. "Oh, I've changed all right. After you left the house I was forced into early retirement—at the ripe old age of twenty-six!"

As Kanae well knew. After her divorce, the leadership of her family—the Hasegawas, who had served as personal bodyguards to the Tokugawa rulers since the time of the sixth shogun, Ienobu—had passed to Ryônosuke's twenty-two-year-old cousin.

"Business is booming as usual, I see."

Through the gap in the shoji, Ryônosuke had evidently caught a glimpse of Kanae's desk. His smile twisted into a frown. Kanae stood up without saying anything, unsure whether to ask him to leave or to invite him inside. In any case, she thought she had better put on some water for tea.

"It's funny, I always knew that some men get dealt a losing hand in life—but I never thought it would be me!" Ryônosuke's voice filled every corner of the room. "You know that commander's son you were once engaged to?" he continued. "He took the money my father gave him and started dealing in secondhand goods. Now he's got his own shop and two or three employees. And to think he might have ended up the son-in-law of an impoverished shogunal retainer! Boy, do I envy him!"

Kanae had no reply. Eight years before, her father, Hasegawa Shimanosuke, had sold his commission in the bodyguards for five hundred *ryô* in cash to a Nihonbashi pawnbroker by the name of Katsutaya Denbei—Ryônosuke's father. As part of the bargain, he had agreed to adopt Ryônosuke as the Hasegawa family's heir.

Shimanosuke had gotten deep into debt through caring for his ailing wife. After her death, he had found himself unable to pay off the steadily mounting interest on his loans, much less the principal. The rice broker who held his debts had even gone so far as to place a lien on his annual stipend of seventy bales of rice, leaving him virtually penniless.

Kanae had been sixteen at the time and, as Ryônosuke had said, was betrothed to the second son of Shimanosuke's superior, the commander of the shogunal guards. When the engagement was broken off Kanae had expected the young man to be devastated, but in fact he had withdrawn with surprising alacrity upon being offered one-fifth of the sum Denbei was to pay Shimanosuke for his commission. Rather than scrape by as a shogunal retainer on the same paltry stipend his ancestors had been receiving for generations, he had chosen to open a business and live by his wits as a merchant. So he'd thrown away his sword and used Denbei's money to open a secondhand goods store. But to merchants like Denbei and Ryônosuke, the title of "samurai" held an irresistible allure.

As a condition of buying Shimanosuke's commission, Denbei had stipulated that Shimanosuke put Kanae up for adoption. His reasoning was that sooner or later Ryônosuke would want to marry, and if Kanae were still living at home, there might be friction between her and Ryônosuke's bride. Shimanosuke had no choice but to accept Denbei's terms. Thus, Kanae found herself adopted by Katsutaya Denbei's younger brother, also a pawnbroker.

Then, on a visit to his uncle's house, Ryônosuke had met Kanae and fallen in love. In order for Kanae, now the daughter of a merchant, to marry Ryônosuke, now the son of a samurai, she had to be adopted again, this time by one of her father's colleagues. Thus, by this complex and circuitous route Kanae had returned to the Hasegawa home as Ryônosuke's bride.

For a while everything had seemed to be going well, and the first two years of their marriage passed uneventfully. But what with paying off his debts and the obligatory gratuities to his superiors for various favors, the money Shimanosuke had received from Ryônosuke's father slowly dwindled. He began taking in piecework to make ends meet. That was when Ryônosuke's mood had turned sour.

All samurai families were beset by financial problems. It was unavoidable given that the stipend they received from the government was fixed, regardless of how much prices rose. Lower-ranking samurai like those in the shogunal guards had long since abandoned their pretensions and their pride, throwing their energies into odd jobs to earn a bit of extra cash. Some sweated over tree nurseries or made paper kites, while others raised crickets or goldfish. Shimanosuke's sideline was copying manuscripts and writing letters on behalf of people from out of town involved in legal proceedings in the capital. It was relatively good work and many samurai in Shimanosuke's circle of acquaintances envied him for it.

Nevertheless, Ryônosuke, with his reverence for the privileged status of the samurai, thought it degrading for his father-in-law to be moonlighting in this way. Many a time he had told Shimanosuke that if it were money he needed, the Katsutayas would come to his aid. But Shimanosuke had steadfastly refused. As far as he was concerned, having sold his commission to a merchant it was now out of the question to turn around and accept charity.

At the time, Kanae had thought her father's feelings were entirely justified. But now, looking back, she understood how Ryônosuke must have felt, sitting there night after night drinking saké with a sullen expression on his face, and why, in the end, his behavior had turned violent. Could one blame him, what with his father-in-law devoting all his energies to his second job, and his own wife, with her beautiful handwriting, helping out from time to time? Then there was his colleague in the shogunal guards, formerly the son of a cloth wholesaler, who happily spent his time raising and selling crickets. Amidst such industriousness, Ryônosuke must have felt that he stood out like a sore thumb.

Shimanosuke had simply gone about his work, watching Ryônosuke out of the corner of his eye as the young man seethed with anger. To make matters worse, he took any job that was offered him, so Kanae was roped into helping out more and more. Ryônosuke would fly into a rage whenever he saw Kanae and Shimanosuke sitting together talking, even when they weren't working.

Once he had picked up Kanae's desk and thrown it into the garden. "Get out!" he had screamed, brandishing his sword. That had been four years earlier, when he had discovered the head clerk from the Tsuruya in the house consulting Kanae about a job. She had told Ryônosuke that she intended to refuse the clerk's request, and that she had no interest in doing any more than was necessary to help her father, but Ryônosuke's anger was not assuaged.

"Do as you like!" he had said. "Copy your documents and your letters if it pleases you. I'm going back to my father to get some money so I can live comfortably. Heaven knows I'm no good for anything else!"

Fearful for his life, the Tsuruya's head clerk had scurried off, followed shortly by Kanae, who left the house with only the clothes on her back. Kanae had found the clerk waiting for her outside the front gate. At his urging, she had taken refuge at the Tsuruya for the night.

The next day, Ryônosuke had not even sent a messenger to track her down. Instead, Shimanosuke and Denbei came by the Tsuruya in person to speak to her. She was not sure what sort of agreement the two men had struck, but they had ordered her to return home—that is, to Denbei's younger brother's house—while Ryônosuke, whose violent behavior had become the subject of gossip, was forced to cede leadership of the Hasegawa family to his cousin and go into retirement.

But Kanae had not returned home. Instead, she had insisted on living alone and enlisted Kiemon's help in renting a house for herself. She took in calligraphy work and even a little letter-writing—which she did not particularly care for on the side. Two years later her father had appeared on her doorstep carrying a bundle. "I've turned all the family's affairs over to him," Shimanosuke had muttered as he threw his bundle down on the floor—

"Hey!" Ryônosuke's voice brought Kanae out of her reverie. "How long are you going to let the tea sit there steeping?"

Kanae hurriedly took the lid off the earthenware teapot, which her hand had been resting on since she had filled it with hot water. Inside the leaves had soaked up as much water as they could hold.

"I'm sorry, the spout's blocked . . ." Kanae muttered desultorily as she got up and went to the kitchen, where she emptied the sodden leaves into a bamboo sieve and began washing out the pot.

"My adoptive son's getting married, you know." Ryônosuke's voice sounded surprisingly near.

Kanae took a moment to compose herself before turning around. Sure enough, Ryônosuke had followed her through the tatami room and was now standing in the doorway of the kitchen, his eyes fixed on her.

"You've probably heard that he's a dead serious type. Apparently his superiors think very highly of him."

"But that's good, isn't it?"

Ryônosuke smiled wryly. "I had big ambitions, too, you know, when your family adopted me." Not knowing what to say, Kanae picked up a dishtowel and began drying the teapot. "I'd heard the guards division was an easy stepping stone to the bookkeeping office, where I'd have more clout than a common rank-and-file samurai. So I decided to use my old man's money to buy myself a promotion. Then I'd really be able to make you and your father happy."

"That's a very kind sentiment."

"Yeah, but the times had changed—it wasn't as easy as it once was to get a place in the bookkeeping office. I was told that unless you knew someone high up in the castle or had lots of money, you didn't stand a chance."

Their eyes met. Filled with a sudden, awful premonition, Kanae drew away from him. In the cramped kitchen, however, there was little room for her to maneuver. Ryônosuke grabbed her by the sleeve and pulled her down as though delivering a karate chop. He had been trained in the martial arts since childhood, and was far stronger than she had imagined.

"Please stop it! What about your young wife you married only the year before last?"

"She's not my wife—she's just a woman who looks after me."

"Liar!"

Ryônosuke's lips ran across the nape of Kanae's neck as she struggled desperately to get free of him. The teapot she had been holding must have caught on something for it fell onto the floor near her feet and shattered. At that moment, she heard the sound of someone calling from the front door.

"Miss Rikô? It's Iguchi Tôi. I just stopped by on an errand . . ."

For a brief moment, Ryônosuke relaxed his grip. Pushing him away with all her might, Kanae fled into the small three-mat room.

Through the shoji between the tatami room and the hallway, which had been left open, Kanae saw Tôi standing inside the front door.

Kanae hurriedly straightened her disheveled hair and adjusted her collar, but she was at a loss as to how to greet her visitor. Tôi sat down on the floor of the hall. If he had noticed anything amiss in her demeanor, his expression betrayed nothing. Ryônosuke's straw sandals lay at his feet. Kanae felt beads of sweat standing out on her back and chest.

"I've just come from Master Tanehiko's house. I shamelessly went to ask for his assistance in getting my book published," he said, staring out through the lattice of the front door. "In return for giving his consent, he asked me to deliver this to you."

From the breast of his kimono he pulled a manuscript covered with writing and neatly drawn illustrations. He turned to look at Kanae just as she was wiping the sweat from her brow with the edge of her sleeve.

"Thank you for taking the trouble to come all this way."

"Well, that's all I came about—but since I'm here, would you care to step outside with me for a little while?"

Apparently he had suspected something untoward had happened in the kitchen and was giving her a chance to get away. But just then they heard Ryônosuke's voice from the other room.

"There's no need for that," he said as he emerged from the kitchen into the three-mat room licking blood from one of his fingers, which he must have cut during their struggle, perhaps on the nail that held the bamboo sieve. "I'm leaving." With as much bravado as he could muster, Ryônosuke strode out of the room and into the hall without so much as a glance at Kanae. There he stopped and looked at Tôi, who had risen to his feet.

"Aren't you Iguchi Shizume of the castle armory?" Ryônosuke asked.

"That is indeed the name my father gave me," Tôi said, looking away. "I'm afraid I can't recall where we've met."

"You wouldn't!" Ryônosuke said, bursting into laughter. "It was around the time I was adopted by Kanae's family. I saw you on Izumibashi Street near the Hasegawa residence. Only the friend I was with pulled me aside so you wouldn't see us. He told me, 'That guy likes to pick fights with former merchants like us who've become samurai— watch out for him!' I saw you once again after that, but of course I hid until you'd gone past."

"I'm sorry about your friend," Tôi said, his smile turning into a frown. "But it wasn't I who picked that quarrel."

"I heard your father had disinherited you and adopted a new heir from a rich merchant family, leaving you high and dry."

"That is true."

"Later I heard you'd taken the pen name Ôtei Mitsuhiko and become Tanehiko's protégé—then you got thrown out of your father's house for drawing your sword. The only reason the authorities didn't get involved was that your father's new heir used his family's money to hush the incident up."

"That is also true," Tôi replied. "But the man I wounded wasn't the scoundrel who bought his samurai status from my family—it was my own father."

"Really? So you crossed swords with your old man!"

"I couldn't bear to see him sponging off his new relatives, getting drunk and chasing women—everything he'd always wanted to do when we were poor." Ryônosuke said nothing. "I didn't mean to hurt him. He was holding a pair of fire tongs—I thought he would ward off my blow, but he didn't move."

Kanae recalled having heard about the incident. A retired officer in the castle armory was said to have fallen and gotten scraped up. There were rumors he had actually been struck by a sword and that his attacker was none other than his own son, whom he had disinherited. However, a woman who happened to witness the incident claimed that the old man had tripped while holding a razor and that the wound was only a slight cut. Nothing ever came of it and eventually the rumors had fizzled out.

"I stormed out of the house," Tôi continued. "But then, not long afterward, my father came to see me. That was a shock!" he said with a rueful smile. "Asked me to hire him as a servant! Well, I begged him to go back home, saying I'd send for him when I was better established as a writer. He's still waiting."

"My case is exactly the opposite," Ryônosuke said, shrugging his shoulders. "As you can see, I've been forced to give up my position and retire. My father, on the other hand, opened an import store about five years ago. Says in a couple more years he's going to buy himself a haberdashery wholesaler's license. Isn't that a fine how-do-you-do!"

"Well, you know what they say," responded Tôi. "Desire for success consumes eight-tenths of a man's energies. But if one has no prospect of success, where does a man devote his energies?" The image of his father, sick of scraping by on a stipend of thirty bales of rice, selling his shogunal commission and doing exactly as he pleased, seemed to flash through his mind. The smile on his face vanished.

If Tôi's father's only ambition was to see his son become a best-selling writer, then what, Kanae wondered, did her own father have to look forward to? She thought of how Shimanosuke had gone round to the Tsuruya to see Kiemon for the first time after moving in with her. Apparently he had gone behind Kanae's back and told Kiemon he would be taking over her copying work. Thereafter, whenever Masukichi came by with a manuscript to be copied, he stipulated that the work was for Kanae. It was then she had thought of quitting altogether.

"I'm going," said Ryônosuke.

"I've outstayed my welcome, too," added Tôi.

The clattering of the lattice door echoed unusually loudly in Kanae's ears.

⁂

Several days later, Masukichi came round to drop off Tôi's manuscript of *A Traveler's Dream on a Grass Pillow*. All of a sudden, Kiemon had decided to go ahead and publish it. Utagawa Kunisada, the popular artist who was illustrating all of Tanehiko's *Fake Murasaki*, had agreed to do the pictures. It seemed Tanehiko had kept up his end of the bargain.

Masukichi left after passing on Kiemon's instructions that Kanae work with all possible speed. Publication was set for the next New Year—the same as the latest installment of *The Fake Murasaki*—but the carver had said he wanted to get Tôi's book out of the way before starting on Tanehiko's. Perhaps he intended to squeeze it in between other more important jobs. He must have guessed from Kiemon's sour expression that he was unenthusiastic about publishing *A Traveler's Dream* and was only doing it to accommodate Tanehiko.

"That's a relief in any case," Kanae thought to herself.

Still kneeling in the entrance hall after seeing Masukichi off at the front door, Kanae casually opened up Tôi's manuscript. The sketches in Tôi's own hand were far better than Kanae would have imagined, perhaps as good as anything Kunisada could do. There was a picture of a geisha and the vigilante hero of the story standing together under an umbrella, looking scornfully at the apparent villain. There was something about Tôi's depiction of the vigilante that reminded her of him.

"Another job from Kiemon?"

It was her father's voice. Kanae looked over her shoulder and saw Shimanosuke standing there, holding something flat wrapped up in cloth. He was going out to make a delivery, having gotten a wooden board from the carpenter across the street so that he could carry his calligraphy paper without it getting crumpled. Yesterday he had said something about a job from a pharmaceutical supplier, so perhaps he had been copying out the names of medicinal powders to be printed onto paper envelopes.

When Shimanosuke had been without any work at all, he had often made Kanae get up from her desk to get dinner ready or to prepare tea for him straight after Masukichi had dropped off a manuscript for her, knowing full well that she stayed up late at night slaving over her work. But that no longer happened now that he was getting jobs of his own writing letters and drawing children's games. Perhaps these jobs were enough to assuage the humiliation he felt over being looked after by his daughter, and his bitterness over seeing his work go to her. Or maybe the piece of wood from the carpenter was just a ploy to show off how meticulous he was compared to Kanae, who was prone to submitting her work late. Perhaps it was a sign of his sense of superiority.

"Tanehiko again?" he asked, peering over her shoulder at the manuscript Kanae held in her hands. "He's been publishing a lot."

"No, this is by someone called Iguchi Tôi."

For some reason, Kanae felt herself blush. This unexpected reaction to saying Tôi's name left her feeling somewhat confused. She thought Shimanosuke would start questioning her about what she knew about the author, but instead he simply said, "Never heard of him," and went out through the front door.

Kanae returned to her room and resumed looking over Tôi's manuscript. The first chapter was set in Edo on the road between Nihonbashi and Shinagawa. The picture she had been looking at a moment earlier depicted a scene where the heroine, a geisha recently betrothed to the son of a wealthy cotton merchant, is rescued from the clutches of the villain. Her fiancé is in Osaka learning the family business and, taking advantage of his absence from Edo, her brother-in-law had turned her over to the villain to pay off a loan. It is then that the vigilante steps in and whisks her away proclaiming, "I am the one she has promised to marry!" The climax of the story was the tearful separation at Shinagawa between the vigilante and another young woman who has fallen in love with him. He must accompany the geisha to Osaka to fulfill a debt he owes her fiancé, but the young woman mistakenly believes that the two are lovers. He leaves without being able to tell her the truth.

Both the young woman's anguish and the geisha's innermost feelings were described in a prose style dripping with pathos and emotion, and Kanae was sure that when it was published it would prove very popular with female readers.

The next day, Masukichi returned with a message for Kanae to come to the Tsuruya immediately and to bring Tôi's manuscript with her.

Kanae had been rubbing a stick of ink on her inkstone, but stopped what she was doing and rushed over. Kiemon was waiting for her in the small room at the bottom of the stairs.

"What——?"

"Look at this!"

Kiemon placed several sheets of paper on the floor in front of her. It was a draft of chapters eight through ten of Tanehiko's new installment of *The Fake Murasaki,* the beginning of which Kanae had already been given to copy. She quickly glanced over the pages and then looked at Kiemon.

He returned her gaze. "Aren't they similar?" he asked.

"Aren't what similar?"

"*The Fake Murasaki* and *A Traveler's Dream,*" Kiemon retorted. "It was careless of me not to read it before sending it to you to copy. I had a shock when it came back and I looked at it for the first time."

Kanae remained silent. She didn't know what Kiemon was trying to say.

"You're the only one who's read *A Traveler's Dream* apart from the publisher's guild. So let me ask you something, okay? In Tanehiko's story Prince Genji saves the princess from the clutches of Yamana Sôzen by pretending to be her lover. In Tôi's story the vigilante rescues the geisha, again by pretending to be her lover. Don't they seem similar to you?"

"Well, when you put it like that they are rather similar . . ."

In terms of style, though, the two books were completely different. *The Fake Murasaki* seemed to call for gaudy, colorful illustrations, while *A Traveler's Dream* was suited to simple, monochromatic ink drawings.

"But surely the guild officer didn't find them to be similar?"

Kiemon shook his head. "The guild is always very lenient. But if we want Nishimura Eijudô to publish it—now that's a different matter."

"Why won't the Tsuruya publish it?"

Kiemon heaved a deep sigh. "Look, try to imagine what would happen. Two books about a hero who rescues a woman by pretending to be her lover, both with illustrations by Kunisada, both released at New Year's, and both for sale side by side on our shelves!" Kiemon sounded weary.

Evidently he would have preferred to have nothing to do with a work of fiction by an unknown writer of dubious commercial viability. He had agreed to publish Tôi's work based solely on Tanehiko's recommendation, something he almost certainly would have avoided if it hadn't been for the fact that *The Fake Murasaki* had revived the Tsuruya's fortunes. If publication of *A Traveler's Dream* were to be suspended over this, it would be some time before any book of Tôi's appeared on a book merchant's shelves.

After four years of copying manuscripts, however, Kanae's instincts told her that *A Traveler's Dream* would be as big a commercial success as *The Fake Murasaki*. Not only did it have a plot full of twists and turns, but it also was an ingenious parody of the old legend of Oguri Hangan and Princess Terute—with a young merchant learning the tools of his trade in Osaka standing in for Oguri, and the geisha who goes in pursuit of him as Princess Terute. And with illustrations by Kunisada, it was just the sort of book that would appeal to patrons of lending libraries. Once it had gained a devoted following, many people would want to buy it as a gift.

"By the way," said Kiemon, "how far have you got in the copying?"

"I'm almost done," lied Kanae without batting an eyelash. "After all, you did say it was urgent."

"What a mess!" Kiemon said, clasping his forehead dramatically. "I'm terribly sorry, but would you mind accepting half your fee for as much as you've done so far?"

"Half . . . ?" Kanae replied, putting on her most troubled expression. "But I was counting on that money."

"Yes, I know. However, I can't afford to pay the entire copying fee for a book that's not going to be published—"

"In that case, why not go ahead and publish it? It's been approved by the guild."

"That's easy for you to say!"

"I rely on this work for my livelihood. It puts me in a most awkward position when you say you don't need a manuscript I've almost finished working on. Can't you find *some* way to publish it?"

"There's nothing I can do," Kiemon replied. Then, much to her surprise he added, "But since it's you and not just anyone, I'm willing to pay two-thirds of your fee."

Kanae saw Tôi's prospects of becoming an established writer recede into oblivion. That ambition of his which consumed eight-tenths of his energies would now certainly flicker and go out.

"Wait a minute!" she cried, excitedly grabbing the hem of Kiemon's kimono. "What if he rewrites it . . . the scene at Shinagawa? Could you publish it then?"

"What's that?"

"We'll ask Tôi to change a few things. If the vigilante explains his situation to the young woman, that would alter the story."

"But the publishing guild—"

"With all the books being published these days, no one at the guild is going to remember the plot of *A Traveler's Dream*. And even if someone did, you could just say the copyist made a mistake."

Kiemon looked doubtfully at Kanae, who was still clutching his kimono. Then he gave a slight nod of consent.

"Now that I think of it," he said, "it was Tôi who delivered Tane-hiko's manuscript to you, wasn't it?" He smiled and looked away from Kanae, whose face had turned bright red. Then he added, "I'll give him three more days."

"Thank you!"

Kanae bowed deeply and made to leave the room while Kiemon's face was still turned away. From over her shoulder she heard him call, "Remember—three days! I've already gone and given the carver another job to do. And as for Master Kunisada, you know how busy he is. If Tôi's job gets delayed it'll cause trouble for everyone!"

"Okay."

On her way out of the Tsuruya, Kanae asked Masukichi where she could find Tôi and dashed off.

It turned out that Tôi lived in Shin-Izumichô not far from her own neighborhood. She soon found the house she was searching for. The front door was unlocked but all the rain shutters had been lowered. Kanae went next door to the neighbor's house. A woman stuck her head out the door and informed her that Tôi had gotten up unusually early that morning and shuttered up the house, saying he was off to Odawara.

A feeling of despair descended over Kanae. If Tôi had gone just about anywhere else—even the Yoshiwara pleasure quarters—Kanae would have chased after him, gotten him to change his manuscript, and then dashed back to the Tsuruya. But even if she went all the way to Odawara it would probably take three days just to track him down.

"It seems he's getting a book published," the neighbor continued. "He said the next one's going to be set on the road between Oiso and Odawara, and he went off in high spirits. Funny—he's usually such an unfriendly man," she mused, raising her hand to her mouth.

Distractedly, Kanae thanked her and turned on her heels.

⟶⟵

Having rewritten about half of the Shinagawa episode, Kanae put down her brush.

Perhaps I should just give up.

She knew Tôi wouldn't be pleased by what she was doing. After all, she would be upset if Shimanosuke were to rewrite something of *hers* without her permission. But if the Tsuruya had come up with such a flimsy excuse not to publish *A Traveler's Dream,* it was a sure bet that any future publisher Tôi sought out for his next book would do likewise.

If this opportunity slipped away it would be a long time before any book of Tôi's ever got published. Kanae was certain it would be a bestseller if it were published, but until then no other publishing house would be willing to take a chance on him.

There's nothing to do but rewrite that scene.

Kanae picked up her brush again and dipped it in ink. Then she pictured Tôi's face wracked with anger. *Why don't you mind your own business!* she imagined him yelling at her. *I don't want to be published if it means getting help from some copyist!* he would say, tearing what she'd written into pieces, balling it up, and throwing it on the floor.

"I might as well . . ."

Give up.

Kanae wiped the tip of her brush across an old piece of paper to remove the excess ink and replaced the lid on the box containing her inkstone. Her hand rested on the lid. If she stopped now the manuscript of *A Traveler's Dream* would be worth no more than the old paper she used for wiping her brushes.

Falteringly, Kanae took the lid off the inkstone box. No matter how great a masterpiece *A Traveler's Dream* might be, it wasn't worth a single copper if no one ever got the chance to read it.

Kanae again dipped her brush in ink.

⟶⟵

"Miss Rikô! Miss Rikô!" It was Masukichi's voice. It sounded as though he was running down the street calling out her name.

Wiping her hands on her apron, Kanae started to move from the kitchen into the three-mat room. Just then she heard what sounded like Masukichi colliding with the lattice door as he raced into the house.

"What is it? Why are you in such a hurry?"

"Something terrible has happened," he said breathlessly. "Mr. Tôi is furious—he left the Tsuruya in a huff saying he had a score to settle with Master Tanehiko."

"What?"

"It looked like he'd just returned from a trip—he was still wearing his wristbands and leggings. After talking to the boss for a while he just flew into a rage and—"

It seemed that Tôi had been shown Kanae's revised manuscript of *A Traveler's Dream* and had mistakenly assumed it was Tanehiko's doing. Kiemon had tried to explain the situation to him, but he had been too hotheaded to listen and had charged out of the shop. Kanae herself didn't wait for Masukichi to finish speaking before rushing out of the house.

Ryûtei Tanehiko was just a pen name; the author's real name was Takaya Hikoshirô and he was a high-ranking shogunal retainer with an income of two hundred bales of rice and an official residence in Okachimachi in Shitaya. Kanae's own family home—where Ryôno-suke now lived—was not far away.

To get there she crossed Izumibashi Bridge. She had no time to take a roundabout route in order to avoid the possibility of running into Ryônosuke, so instead she proceeded along Izumibashi Street, keeping her face hidden behind the sleeve of her kimono.

From a distance she could see the white wall with black cross-hatching that surrounded the estate of Lord Katô of the Ôzu clan from Iyo province. Tanehiko's residence was just beyond it. She had heard that Tanehiko had originally been given an official residence in a less desirable neighborhood near the canal in the south part of Honjo, but that he had moved to Okachimachi claiming the location would make it easier for him to fulfill his duties.

The residence's main gate consisted of a small building with a guard post on one side, although there was no guard on duty now. The small gate, which one had to crouch to pass through, had been left open as usual. As Kanae entered she heard a man's voice speaking loudly. It sounded like Tôi.

When she reached the front door, Kanae called out but got no response. Neither the servant who always seemed to be pulling weeds in the garden when Kanae had come before, nor any of Tanehiko's disciples who usually greeted visitors at the door, was anywhere to be seen. She heard Tôi's voice again, only louder this time. Hurriedly, Kanae went around to the side of the house.

The house itself wasn't all that large, and when she opened the bamboo gate into the garden she found herself outside the drawing room. Inside the dimly lit room, cut off from the sun by the house's long overhanging eaves, Tôi sat with the dust of his journey still clinging to his hair. On the floor lay the rewritten manuscript, which he struck with his fist as he berated Tanehiko.

"Who did you tell to rewrite this? More to the point, what was wrong with my story that you had to go and make a mess of it?"

"Please calm down. All I told Kiemon was that your book was worth publishing."

"In that case, where did this come from?"

"From me." It was Kanae who spoke.

Tôi looked at her. Tanehiko also turned to her with a look in his eye that seemed to ask, where did *she* appear from? Kanae nodded deferentially toward Tanehiko before turning her gaze on Tôi.

"I . . . I was the one who rewrote your manuscript."

"Why?"

Faltering from time to time, Kanae explained what had happened. She told him everything—including how she had gone to his house only to find him away and how, after much doubt and hesitation, she had rewritten his story. Tôi listened to her quietly, biting his lip.

Kanae knelt down on the step and bowed deeply. "Forgive me. When I heard that unless it was rewritten Kiemon wouldn't publish it, I—"

"In that case, the best thing to do would have been to publish it under your own name." Tôi raised his head and looked up at the ceiling. "That's no longer my work."

"That's not true! I could never write a story as good as that."

"In that case, why did you interfere?" Tôi flung the folded manuscript toward her. It landed softly on the step. "This is worse than getting slapped in the face—but I guess a mere copyist like you wouldn't understand that."

"I do understand," Kanae said, her voice cracking. Tôi looked away, his mouth twisted into a frown. "You see, I want to be better than anyone else, too."

Tôi didn't reply.

"Even if it means I have so much work that I have to stay up all night, I want people to hire me and not anyone else. I want them to say, 'This story is really good—make sure Miss Rikô copies it.' The other day when I heard you say ambition was eight-tenths of a man, I knew exactly what you meant."

"Eight-tenths a man?" Tanehiko asked, puzzled.

Kanae ignored him and continued, "Please forgive me—I know what I did was presumptuous. But if *A Traveler's Dream* doesn't get published, I thought . . ."

At last she burst into tears. A series of images flashed through her mind. Tôi, disgusted with himself for not having the wherewithal to take in his father when he came asking to be hired as a servant; her own father, Shimanosuke, who assuaged his disappointment by copying out children's games; and Ryônosuke, forced to sit on the sidelines watching his cousin and his wife run the house.

The wind blew Tôi's manuscript off the step. It landed on the ground.

She thought she heard Tôi murmur something that sounded like, "I'm sorry."

"Right, then." It was Tanehiko's voice. "Personally, I can't make head or tail of any of this, but it seems you two have reached some sort of agreement so I'm going out."

Tôi mumbled some sort of acknowledgement.

"Look after things while I'm gone," continued Tanehiko. "Anyway, the servant should be back soon."

Kanae looked up, partially shielding her face with her sleeve. Tanehiko was standing on the veranda gazing up at the sky, even though there wasn't the least sign of rain.

III

᠀ NO TIME FOR TEARS ᠀

Takemoto Kosen, the headlining *jôruri* performer of the evening, came to the end of her rendition of *The Saké Shop*.

The audience was silent.

Kosen lowered her eyes and remained kneeling motionless on her cushion for a moment before putting down her samisen. An irrepressible smile rose to her lips as she placed her hands on the floor before her and bowed deeply. The audience erupted into applause.

Without waiting for the ovation to die down, the woman announcer, who doubled as a fortune-teller during intermissions, thanked the audience for coming. Backstage, Oen left the dressing room together with the third singer on the program, Takemoto Masukiyo, and went out into the corridor. Oen's stage name was Takemoto Shichino-suke—though everyone just called her "Oshichi." That evening she had performed the ballad of *Nozaki Village* right before Kosen had gone on. Masukiyo had sung first, being what was known in *jôruri* circles as a *habakatari,* or "lead-in" performer. As Oen emerged from the stuffy dressing room, a young man opened a window near the top of the stairs and she felt a cool breeze waft over her body.

Even at full capacity the Momozonotei, a vaudeville theater in Shiba just around the corner from the Shinmei Shrine, could seat no more than a hundred. Part of the audience had spilled out into the corridor during the performance. Now men were streaming down the narrow staircase two and three abreast, lolling their heads from side to side as though trying to relieve the stiffness in their shoulders brought on by having had their attention riveted on the performance, or perhaps simply due to having been packed so tightly together inside the hall.

Oen scoured the crowd for familiar faces, thanking those she recognized. Silver chains dangled from her ornamental hairpins, swaying back and forth as she bowed again and again. Suddenly she felt conscious of smiling a little too much, and pursed her lips.

The Momozonotei's "girls' *jôruri*" performance featuring Kosen as *shinkatari*—the star attraction—had begun two days before, on July 2, and was due to run two more days, until the sixth. A buzz had started to build around the event as soon as the flyers had been distributed the previous month. Though everyone had been expecting a good turnout, no one was prepared for the size of the crowds that showed up. The evening before they had been unable to squeeze everyone into the hall, even after asking people to hold their smoking boxes on their laps, and the overflow crowd had spilled out onto the stairs.

Kosen seemed convinced that she alone was responsible for the huge turnout. Oen, on the other hand, suspected it was not the gorgeous diva known as the "Singing Komachi," after a ninth-century poetess of renowned beauty, that a majority of the audience had come to see. When the two women had appeared together at another vaude-ville theater in May, one samurai who had come especially to hear Kosen had gone away Oen's devoted fan.

Tonight, several men in the audience—country samurai serving in Edo from the look of them—had applauded loudly at the end of Oen's rendition of *Nozaki Village*. As she left the stage, she had seen them stand up, pick their way through the packed hall, and leave. Perhaps they had simply been in a hurry to get back to their lords' estates before curfew. And yet, if they had really come especially to see Kosen, surely they could have slipped the night watchman a few coins to let them in by a side gate after hours? No, Oen was sure they had come just to see her.

A few hangers-on remained in the corridor, even chatting with Masukiyo while hoping to attract Oen's attention. Once the last of them had disappeared down the stairs and the foyer at the bottom had fallen quiet, Oen placed her hands on Masukiyo's shoulders and steered her back toward the dressing room. As they entered, Kosen, who had been there since the end of her performance, shot Oen a glance.

"I wish *I* had such loyal fans, Oshichi. Yours don't even bother to stick around once you're through singing!" she said almost to herself, a faint smile playing about her lips. Kosen left the room, and soon Oen heard the sound of her footsteps descending the stairs. Apparently she was going outside to flirt with the men that always loitered around the theater after a performance.

Such was the enthusiasm of the samurai class for girls' *jôruri* in those days that a popular singer would have no shortage of admirers, powerful *hatamoto* among them, who were more than willing to escort her home after a performance. There was even a popular song that went:

> *Unlike the lord's attendants*
> *The singer's entourage*
> *Never shirks its duty!*

Yet for the past two evenings fewer samurai than usual had volunteered to walk alongside Kosen's palanquin. She had acted unperturbed, but to Oen it was clear she was secretly annoyed. She imagined Kosen stepping out into the street that evening hoping to corral any man about to leave and rope him into joining her retinue.

Oen removed the stiff-shouldered vest she wore over her kimono while performing. She was about to change out of her kimono when she suddenly realized that Ofuyu, who was normally seated in the corner of the dressing room waiting to assist her, was nowhere to be seen. Oen smiled ruefully to herself. Looking around, she spotted the familiar cloth bundle that contained her change of clothes, and picked it up.

Until last year, Oen and Ofuyu had been fellow students. Before becoming Oen's personal assistant, the younger girl had even performed several times under the stage name Kamenosuke. Back then she had had one particularly ardent admirer named Kishimoto, if Oen's memory served her correctly, who was the second son of a *hata-moto*. Evidently she was still seeing him.

Oen had just finished changing and combing her hair when she heard the sound of footsteps coming up the stairs. It was Ofuyu, who muttered an apology about having stepped outside for a moment and whispered into Oen's ear, "That young gentleman who came the other night is here again asking for you."

"Which one?" Oen said, tilting her head to one side.

Ofuyu covered her mouth with both hands and giggled as though she had just recalled something funny. "You know, the one with the nose . . ."

"Oh, you mean that guy from up north?" Oen, too, gave a playful giggle.

Toward the end of the previous month, a clothier in Owarichô had invited Oen to dine with him at a restaurant in Negishi. There she had met two samurai from Shinjô, a fief in northeastern Japan. Oen was already acquainted with one of the men, who looked after his clan's estate in Edo while his lord was away. The other had just arrived in the capital a month earlier. At twenty-four, he was seven years older than Oen, but his face was like a teenager's, all covered with pimples, with one red and swollen boil sitting right on the tip of his nose.

"Today he's put a plaster on it!" Ofuyu was sweating from the exertion of laughing so hard.

"What was his name again? Ishibashi something . . . Matajûrô, wasn't it? Why didn't you just send him away?"

"But," replied Ofuyu, wiping her forehead and regaining her composure, "your appointment with Chôemon isn't until tomorrow."

"You didn't tell that guy I'd see him, did you?"

"No, I said I'd check with you first."

"Uh-huh." Oen got up and went into the hall where the audience sat during performances. Ofuyu followed her.

The seat cushions and ashtrays had been cleared away and somehow the theater looked much smaller now than when it had been full. A fly that must have come in through the window near the top of the stairs buzzed around the sole remaining lantern.

Oen opened a window at the back of the room and looked out. Across from the theater a thicket of trees on the grounds of the Sendai clan's estate was wreathed in darkness. Beneath the window ran the small street that everyone referred to as Hikagechô, where a large number of men were still milling about. One group stood huddled around the lantern hanging above the doorway of the Momozonotei. They appeared to be Kosen's fans. Kosen herself was out of view under the eaves of the building, but Oen could hear her voice. It was saccharine sweet—completely unlike the voice she used when performing.

At a slight remove from this party of men was another small group, no doubt waiting for Oen. Further away still, a man stood alone with his arms crossed. From the window, Oen couldn't make out the sticking plaster on his nose, but judging from his powerful build, evident from the muscular cast of his shoulders prominent beneath his kimono, Oen was sure it was the samurai Ishibashi Matajûrô.

Oen turned and looked at Ofuyu. "Let's go home."

"What about him?" Ofuyu asked.

"Tell him I'm busy tonight, tomorrow night, and the night after that—and every night from now on."

"But—"

"Look, if I gave every man who wanted to see me the time of day, I'd be finished," said Oen, sounding annoyed. She could just imagine how Kosen would laugh at her were she to accept an invitation from a country bumpkin like Ishibashi Matajûrô. "My, what nice fans you have, Oshichi!" she would say with a smile.

⁕

Oen's palanquin had apparently reached the Kakimura restaurant near Ueno's Shinobazu Pond, where Awajiya Chôemon was waiting for her. The palanquin bearers lowered her gently to the ground and called out that they had arrived.

Before leaving the theater, Oen had tried to decline her fans' offers to act as an escort, but seven or eight samurai had nevertheless insisted on accompanying her to the restaurant. As she stepped out of her conveyance, Oen quickly peered at the faces around her in the light of the lanterns outside the restaurant. She was relieved to see not a single sticking plaster in sight.

The previous evening, Ishibashi had been among the throng of samurai that escorted Oen home to Shinmeichô after her performance. Tonight, however, having once again being rebuffed, he had no doubt gone home in a huff. Oen again looked around at her entourage, thanked each man politely, and flashed her most winning smile with its single dimple on one cheek. Seemingly satisfied, the men departed.

Having received generous tips, the palanquin bearers escorted Oen to the entrance of the restaurant, illuminating the path ahead of her with their folding lanterns. When she reached the front door, Oen announced herself in a low voice. At the sound of a reply from inside, the bearers went off, leaving Oen alone.

The proprietress of the Kakimura soon appeared at the door, the skirts of her small-patterned print kimono trailing behind her. As soon as she saw that it was Oen, however, she announced with exaggerated fuss that "Master Chôemon of the Awajiya" would not be coming tonight after all. He had been detained longer than expected in a meeting, she said, and would have to get up early the next morning to leave for Kawasaki on sudden business.

Oen's appointments with Chôemon often turned out this way. To make matters worse, lately his excuses had been riddled with apparent falsehoods.

Oen had it on good authority that the Nihonbashi cosmetics dealer's head had been turned by a woman whom he regularly hired to copy out advertising flyers for his shop. Apparently she was a very proper lady from a samurai family who was not even aware of Chôemon's illicit feelings for her. But in Oen's mind there was no doubt that the copyist was the reason Chôemon's affections toward herself had become somewhat less ardent than before. In the past he would have moved heaven and earth to postpone his trip to Kawasaki a day in order to see her.

Oen glanced back the way she had come. Beyond the front gate was only blackness underneath a starless sky. The bearers' lanterns that had swayed comfortingly in the dark a moment earlier were now gone. She would have to ask the restaurant to call her another palanquin.

As though reading Oen's mind, the proprietress smiled and added, "Don't worry—we'll make sure you get a ride home in the morning."

It was her way of letting Oen know she was welcome to stay in the detached suite she and Chôemon always used when they spent the night together at the restaurant.

Noting the evident relief on Oen's face, the proprietress shrugged her shoulders. "It's the least I can do considering you had to waste your valuable time like this," she said, calling for one of the maids. Oen slipped out of her sandals and went inside.

The suite in question was separated from the rest of the building by a breezeway several feet in length. Oen entered behind the maid and saw that the bedding had already been laid out in the back room half enclosed by a mosquito net.

If Oen were hungry, the maid told her, some food could be brought straight away. Or would she prefer to wash off the sweat of the day? Apparently the bath was also at Oen's disposal. The maid proffered her a small towel and a light cotton kimono.

Since it had been some time since her last rendezvous with Chôemon, Oen had been relishing the opportunity to prove to him she was twice the woman as this Miss Prim-and-Proper of whom he was so enamored. But those plans had come to naught and her nerves were rather frayed.

As Oen plunged into the large cypress wood bathtub brimming with warm soothing water, she felt her tension and fatigue melt away. She rested her arms on the side of the tub and closed her eyes.

In a flash of memory, she recalled how as a child she had rarely enjoyed the luxury of even splashing water on herself, let alone soaking in a tub. Surely neither Oen's real father, who had abandoned her on Nihonbashi Bridge when she was three, nor her adoptive father, who was fond of saying he had found her and taken her home on a drunken lark, could have imagined in their wildest dreams that their little girl would grow up to be escorted in a palanquin by high-ranking samurai to some of Edo's ritziest restaurants.

The young Oen had found herself having to support both herself and her adoptive father, a man with no steady job. She scoured the streets of Edo come rain or snow for bent nails and bits of wire to sell to the scrap dealer. In those days, she was constantly crying from hunger. If any of the neighbors were kind enough to give her a rice ball or a boiled potato she would devour it ravenously. These days, though, it was not uncommon for Oen to leave half of her meal at the Kakimura uneaten.

Oen was six when her adoptive father died. His wife, who had been earning a bit of money peddling hardboiled eggs and soybeans while turning tricks on the side, immediately went and shacked up with a young plasterer. To rid herself of the burdensome Oen, she gave the girl to a young *jôruri* teacher in the neighborhood named Omatsu, extracting the sum of one *ryô* for what she called "the cost of looking after the kid up till now." It would be more accurate to say Oen had been sold.

Omatsu seemed confident that with a little polish something could be made of Oen, with her charming one-dimpled smile. Just as Omatsu had expected, within a month of coming to live with her, Oen put on weight and turned into a most attractive child.

Omatsu trained Oen in her art and went about introducing her to all the theater managers and great *jôruri* masters, hoping to put her newly adopted protégée on the stage. Omatsu had in mind to capitalize on the girls' *jôruri* boom of the early eighteen hundreds sparked by the great female performer Také Somenosuke, who touted it as a form of Confucian filial piety.

It was said that originally girls' *jôruri* had been performed only in private for the likes of daimyo and high-ranking *hatamoto*. Later, patronage of the art passed from the increasingly impoverished warrior class to the nouveau-riche merchants. Girls' *jôruri* became a regular feature of public festivals at temples and shrines. But the wild enthusiasm of *jôruri* fans prompted the authorities to issue a decree banning the practice altogether. Then, during the Bunka era, Somenosuke came along and successfully petitioned for permission to perform on the vaudeville stage so that she could "support her aging mother."

From that moment on, the government's prohibition of girls' *jôruri* was gradually relaxed. It was now 1832, the third year of the Tempo era, and there were said to be nearly two hundred women performing *jôruri* in Edo. Ten years before, when Oen was a child of seven and Omatsu was in her early forties, the number had probably been about the same. What better way for Oen and Omatsu to stand out from the crowd than to put themselves forward as a model of filial piety? Nevertheless, their plans foundered as the young Oen failed to gain much of a following.

Omatsu rehearsed with Oen down by the river late into the night until the girl's throat was raw. She improved to the point where theater managers and veteran performers admitted that she was "pretty good for her age," but audiences were less than enthusiastic. When Oen got up on stage, not even her cute one-dimpled smile, which endeared her to everyone backstage and at home, was enough to make audiences warm to her.

Omatsu pushed Oen harder and harder. She even taught the seven-year-old to cast her eyes coquettishly about the room while she sang. It wasn't until after Omatsu's death that it even occurred to Oen that her teacher's training had been misguided.

Omatsu had died in the fall of 1830, two years ago, when Oen was fifteen. Ironically, it was around that time that Oen's popularity began to grow. With no one around any longer to shout at her all the time, she was free to be herself. Or, to put it in a less positive light, she began to act exactly as she pleased. Oen abandoned her attempts to play samisen and sing ballads in the manner she had been taught. Moreover, as soon as the one hundred days of mourning for Omatsu were over, she took a lover—Chôemon.

Before she died, Omatsu had gone so far as to choose a patron for Oen, a retired lamp oil dealer just shy of fifty. He was certainly no young girl's dream. True, he showed signs of having cut a dashing figure when young, but the wrinkles that showed around his neck when he turned his head made Oen's skin crawl.

Despite Oen's lack of critical acclaim, there had been several other men who had stepped forward to offer themselves as Oen's patron, among them Chôemon and a *hatamoto* with an income of five thousand bushels of rice. But Omatsu had turned them both down. Chôemon, she said, was too fickle for a woman to rely upon, while the *hatamoto* was poor and too proud.

Later, as soon as Oen's romance with Chôemon became serious, the good-natured lamp oil dealer bowed out without a word of complaint. People began referring to Oen as "Chôemon's girl." Now, in hindsight, Oen thought that Omatsu had not been entirely wrong about the cosmetics dealer.

Chôemon had concocted a face lotion called "Moon Dew" that was currently used by just about every young woman in Edo, and had saved his family business from ruin. For a while during his father's day it had looked like the shop might have to be sold, but now there were customers lining up on the street. While some of his fellow merchants admired Chôemon's business acumen, quite a few others despised his cutthroat tactics—such as stealing the formulas of his competitors' products and distributing free samples of Moon Dew outside their shops—and refused to so much as sit down to a meal with him.

Of course, Chôemon had never revealed his true feelings to Oen. Sometimes he would summon her several nights in a row to meet him at the Kakimura, then suddenly there would be no word from him for a whole month. On more than a few occasions she had turned down other invitations due to a prior engagement with Chôemon, only to receive a message just as she was about to leave for the Kakimura that he couldn't make it after all.

Chôemon was in his mid-thirties and in the prime of life, and at first Oen had supposed he simply liked to work hard and play hard. It was only later—just the other day in fact—that something happened to make her realize there was more to it than that.

One evening, too eager even to wait until nightfall, she was preparing to leave for their usual rendezvous at the Kakimura when a message had arrived saying something else had come up. There was nothing much Oen could do about it. She stayed home, had a few drinks, and crawled into bed early, pulling the covers up over her head. A few days later, however, she happened to be at the Kakimura and mentioned it to one of the maids. She was taken aback when the maid told her that Chôemon had indeed come that night, soaked in the bath for a while, and spent the night alone in the detached suite. More-over, on several other occasions lately Chôemon had rushed out in the middle of the evening, saying he had suddenly remembered some matter he needed to discuss with a woman by the name of Hasegawa Rikô.

Nevertheless, Chôemon did not seem to have tired of Oen. Even when she got cross with him he merely laughed it off, and he never failed to send round her monthly allowance. Once she had been so annoyed with him she had looked the other way on passing him in the street, but this had not deterred him from summoning her to the Kakimura the next several nights in a row.

"Don't worry, Miss Oshichi," Ofuyu was always saying to her. "Master Chôemon is very fond of you, even if he does act fickle sometimes." Whether Ofuyu was right or not, there was no denying that Oen needed Chôemon in more ways than one. The fits of anxiety and anger to which his capriciousness drove her lent a certain sensuality to both her singing and her appearance. As time went by, she had more men than even Kosen eager to catch a glimpse of her one-dimpled smile as she alighted from her palanquin and to escort her home.

Oen splashed cold water on her face, which felt flushed, and stepped out of the tub. She slipped into her robe and left the bathroom. On her way back to the detached suite, the maid, having apparently heard Oen getting out of the bath, passed her carrying a dinner tray.

Before entering Oen stopped and stood in the breezeway. The gentle wind blowing between the two buildings felt pleasant on her body.

"Do come in," called the maid, seeing Oen standing motionless in the passageway.

Oen wiped several beads of sweat from between her ample bosom with her damp towel. She was just about to enter the room when she heard a man's voice behind her.

"Hey. It's Shichinosuke, the singer, isn't it?"

It occurred to Oen to pretend not to have heard, but by then she had already turned toward the voice and was smiling her winning smile.

"Long time, no see." The man moved toward her onto the breezeway, stepping into the light of the stone lantern in the garden. She guessed that he was in his early twenties. He wore a crisp kimono of fine Echigo linen, the skirts of which he held up neatly with both hands. "Don't you remember me?" Smiling like a mischievous child, the man craned his neck toward her.

Oen gave a vague nod. He looked familiar but she couldn't put a name to the face.

"You've forgotten, haven't you?" he exclaimed. "How cruel!"

"No, I—"

"That's all right. No need to lie. I've seen you dozens of times at the theater but we've only actually met once."

"Forgive me. I've such a bad memory."

"It must be pretty good to remember all those lyrics! Now then, do you remember entertaining a rice broker and two *hatamoto* here last fall?"

"Why, yes, I do!" Oen exclaimed, clapping her hands.

She remembered him now. His name was Kusutarô, if she wasn't mistaken. His father ran a rice brokerage called the Miyakoya and, as the eldest son, he was being groomed to take over the business. She recalled how he had shrugged sheepishly as he explained to the two samurai upon his arrival that his father had been taken with a sudden fever and had sent him in his stead.

"That can't have been an enjoyable evening for you, I imagine," said Kusutarô, smiling painfully at the memory of it.

"Not at all," Oen replied, shaking her head. In truth, she remembered them all sitting around sipping their saké in dead silence.

The purpose of the meeting at the Kakimura had been to mend fences after the younger of the two samurai had caused a violent scene at a rice brokerage called the Nakataya, to which he owed money.

Now, there wasn't a *hatamoto* in Edo who didn't have debts, a fact many high-ranking samurai bitterly resented. The young *hatamoto* at the Kakimura that night had taken this resentment one step further, declaring that no merchant was going to get rich off of *him* and refusing to repay his loans. "Very well," responded the owner of the Nakataya, "if that's the way you're going to be about it." He then proceeded to impound the young man's government rice stipend.

Enraged, the *hatamoto* had stormed into the Nakataya brandishing his sword. If it had been any other place of business, the owner would probably have fled screaming, but rice brokers were made of sterner stuff. They were accustomed to dealing with samurai and were trained in swordsmanship and judo. Wielding his trusty abacus, the Nakataya's head clerk held the *hatamoto* at bay while the shopkeepers on either side rushed to his aid and succeeded in wresting the samurai's sword away. Seeing as it wouldn't have done anyone any good if the matter were to become public, the owner of the Miyakoya and a senior *hatamoto* intervened, setting up the meeting at the Kakimura to patch things up.

"Tell me," Kusutarô said, moving closer to Oen until their bodies were nearly touching. He lowered his voice. "Who did you come here with tonight?"

"No one, I'm sad to say."

"Don't tell lies." Kusutarô poked her shoulder with his finger.

"I'm not lying."

"If you say so." Kusutarô lowered his voice still further. "How about spending the night with me?"

"You must be joking. Tonight you'll make me happy, tomorrow you'll make me cry—is that it?"

"I'm serious." Kusutarô glanced over Oen's shoulder toward the open doorway of the detached suite. The maid must have gotten up and come over to see what was keeping her. "Some other time, then. Don't be a stranger."

With a warm smile, Kusutarô turned away from Oen and headed off toward one of the other rooms where the sound of a samisen could be heard.

⁓◦◦⁓

From the direction of the stage, Kosen could be heard performing *Ninokuchi Village*.

"She's improved, hasn't she?" said Manbei, the manager of the Momozonotei. "It's funny how popularity can push one to excel, but unpopularity can push one to excel even harder."

Oen smiled but said nothing.

Manbei took a long drag on his pipe and then, once it had gone out, knocked it against the side of the bamboo receptacle beside him to empty out the remains of the shredded tobacco. He was evidently trying to cut down on smoking, having being told by Masukiyo that he smelled like an ashtray. He sucked on the end of his empty pipe for a while but gave up, clearly dissatisfied.

Manbei once again removed the tobacco pouch from where it hung around his waist and began refilling the bowl of his pipe. "Now, this is strictly between you and me . . ." he began, pausing to light his pipe and not bothering to lower his voice. "There's been some talk of promoting you to *shinkatari*."

"Really?" A fire ignited in Oen's brain.

I've done it! she thought. How long had she waited to hear those words? *There, I showed you!* she had the urge to say to no one in particular. Instead she quietly bit her lip.

"But first," Manbei added, "we think you need to improve your samisen playing."

The fire inside Oen's head suddenly went out. She'd been rehearsing quite a bit lately but hadn't yet caught up with Kosen.

Manbei knocked his pipe against the side of the bamboo ashtray and filled it again with tobacco. "You're without a teacher now, Oshichi, whereas Kosen still takes lessons from Senjo. And when it comes to girls your age—women, too, for that matter—a word from Senjo can make or break one's reputation." Before lighting his pipe, Manbei reattached his tobacco pouch to the sash about his waist.

"Sure, Kosen's samisen playing isn't all that great, but what's more important is the bond between master and pupil. When Kosen was promoted to *shinkatari,* Senjo said nothing. But now, even though all the theater owners are in favor of promoting you, they know if they do Senjo will make a fuss about your samisen playing not being good enough." Manbei's fingers fumbled at his waist as he searched again for his tobacco pouch.

But Oen wasn't looking at him anymore. What Manbei was telling her, though not in so many words, was that she needed to curry favor with Senjo—a woman Oen didn't particularly care for. But if that was what it took to become *shinkatari* then that was what she would do.

And that would take money.

Oen bit down on her lip so hard it nearly bled. She would have to get it from Chôemon. But it wouldn't end there. Once she'd become *shinkatari* she would need even more money. Chôemon would have to provide that as well.

Next door, the sound of Kosen's voice and samisen reverberated throughout the room and lingered before dying out. The audience remained quiet for a moment before erupting into applause mixed with scattered cheers. Then the girl who sold fortunes concluded the performance by thanking the audience.

Masukiyo motioned with her eyes to Oen and stood up. Nodding, Oen also rose and went out into the corridor. Perhaps it was her nerves, but deep down she felt drained. As the performers stood in the corridor saying goodbye to their fans, it seemed to Oen that her voice stood out shrilly above the din of the crowd.

With as much grace as she could muster, Oen said a final farewell as the last person descended the stairs. She was about to return to her dressing room when a voice came from downstairs.

"Miss Oshichi!" It was Ofuyu. Her tryst with her boyfriend must again have taken longer than expected, since she came running up the stairs, panting for breath. "That samurai has been here again."

"The one from Shinjô?" Oen asked.

"Yes. He asked me to find out when you'll be able to meet him."

"I thought I told you to tell him to get lost without coming to me about it all the time."

"But he says tonight he's given the night watchman a big tip so it's all right if he stays out a bit late and—"

"Don't be stupid!" Oen suddenly raised her voice. "Do you think I'd waste my time on some poor country bumpkin?"

Taken aback, Ofuyu stared at Oen.

Oen knew she had gone too far, but there was no taking back what she had said. She turned away from Ofuyu with a sullen look.

There was someone standing outside Oen's house when she and Ofuyu returned from their bath at the Umenoyu.

Though the man was facing in their direction, the moonlight shining down from behind him prevented Oen from being able to see his face. Judging from his slender figure, however, it was not Chôemon, and his casual manner of dress was too fashionable for the countrified Ishibashi.

Oen and Ofuyu looked at one another. The man didn't appear to have any sinister intent, but it was entirely possible he was some fan Oen had unintentionally slighted come to confront her.

It was a little past ten o'clock on a summer night and the houses in the neighborhood all had their windows slightly ajar to let in the cool air, so if Oen were to cry out for help people would undoubtedly come running to help her. Nevertheless, fear held her back.

Oen and Ofuyu stopped dead in their tracks. The shadowy figure began moving toward them.

"What are you doing just standing there? This is your house, isn't it?" It was Kusutarô's voice.

With a sigh of relief, Oen rushed up to him. "What are *you* doing here—at this time of night?"

"It's my father. He's gone and cut me off without a cent for squandering my money on a *jôruri* singer named Shichinosuke!" said Kusutarô playfully.

"My, my. What a pity!"

Kusutarô's breath reeked of saké. He must have been drinking quite heavily. Unconcerned that Ofuyu was watching, Kusutarô drew Oen to him and laughed for no apparent reason.

"I've been cast out in the street," he said, "Can I stay with you?"

"What nonsense! Let me call a palanquin to take you home."

"I don't need one. They offered to call me one a little while ago over at that restaurant but I told them not to. I walked."

There were many fancy restaurants lining the street that ran past the Shinmei Shrine. Kusutarô must have been invited to dine at one of them and then, having become overly intoxicated and remembering that Oen lived in the neighborhood, had built up enough courage to walk over to her place.

"There I am, having walked all this way to see you, and some maid sticks her head out your front door and says you're not at home. Well, let me tell you, I was prepared to wait here all night. But what do I find? You've just been at the bathhouse!"

Announcing he was exhausted, Kusutarô, wearing a white cotton kimono with blue cross-hatching and a stiff Hakata obi, plopped himself down on the ground with his legs outstretched. Left to his own devices, Oen thought, he would probably lie down on the ground. But if she tried to help him up, there was the danger he would pull her down on top of him. It would be embarrassing to be seen rolling around in the street with him. Nevertheless, against her better judgment, she held her hand out to Kusutarô. As expected, he grabbed it and pulled her toward him. His breath reeked of alcohol and Oen turned her face away. As she did, Kusutarô caught a whiff of her own clean skin, fresh from the bath.

Oen felt the stubble on Kusutarô's cheek against her face.

"Let's be lovers, Oshichi." They were the same words Chôemon had said to her. "Let's be more than that, if you like," he added.

"Don't tease me."

"I'm not teasing. I fell in love with you the moment I met you last year at the Kakimura."

"I wish I could believe you."

"You can. So let's be lovers. If we're careful, Chôemon will never know."

"No." Oen shook her head, her face buried in Kusutarô's chest. "I want to be more than just your plaything . . ."

Kusutarô's body was soft and supple, quite unlike Chôemon's. There was also something that attracted her about the reckless abandon of a man who didn't care if people saw him sprawled in the street.

As Oen's emotions began to carry her away, the thought of Chôemon's money flashed through her mind.

_＿◌◌＿_

Oen slipped out of the bedding and put on a kimono. As she ran a comb through her disheveled hair, she suddenly found herself softly singing a line from *The Saké Shop*. Something about it had bothered her when she sang it on stage the night before last. She had been thinking that tonight she would have to go over and over it until she was satisfied she'd got it right.

The words seemed to glide smoothly off her tongue. But what would happen when she tried singing it at the top of her voice? Oen suddenly had the urge to pick up her samisen.

She turned and looked at Kusutarô. He was lying on his stomach on the futon. Despite the fact that he didn't smoke, he had opened the drawer of the small smoking chest next to the futon and was playing with the tobacco inside. They were at the teahouse on the island in the middle of Ueno's Shinobazu Pond where they had taken to meeting.

Kusutarô was instantly aware of Oen's gaze, and turned over on his back to look at her. "Yesterday . . ." He paused, smiling suggestively at Oen. "You saw Chôemon, didn't you?"

"No," Oen lied, clenching her jaw. Kusutarô was right, she had met Chôemon the previous night. He had given her the thirty *ryô* she intended to use to ingratiate herself with Senjo.

"It's no good lying."

"I said I didn't meet him."

"I may not show it, but I'm actually quite jealous, you know," Kusutarô said in a tone that made it hard for Oen to know whether or not he was serious. She was just about to place a decorative comb in her coiffure when he reached out and grabbed her sleeve, exposing her bare arm. "Do you want me to put in a good word for you with that old lady, Senjo?"

Oen's hand froze in midair, holding a hairpin. She turned her entire body toward Kusutarô. "Do you know her?"

"Not personally, but I know a *hatamoto* who used to be her lover. He still takes *jôruri* lessons from her, apparently."

"Oh, please! Could you?" Oen put her hands together imploringly.

"Of course." Kusutarô rolled over and got out of the other side of the futon. "I'll go see him in four or five days."

"Four or five days?" said Oen, raising her voice. She'd expected Kusutarô to say he would go and see the samurai the very next day.

"Look—I can't keep seeing you like this if I don't work like hell the rest of the time. Plus, I have to find time for sword training. And I've got meetings to attend."

"I'm sorry." Notwithstanding her apology, Oen still felt dissatisfied.

Oen's great ambition in life was to be promoted to *shinkatari*. Kusutarô's work was important, too, of course, but Oen wished he would realize that her life's ambition took priority over everything else.

_Oen's palanquin was passing through Shiba. Peeping out between the gaps in the bamboo screen, she glimpsed the familiar sights of Udaga-wachô slowly receding behind them. She was on her way home from visiting Senjo.

Kusutarô's *hatamoto* friend had apparently wasted no time in going to speak to Senjo on Oen's behalf. The *jôruri* teacher had received Oen warmly, happily accepting the money Oen placed in front of her. And when Oen broached the subject of being promoted to *shinkatari,* Senjo promised not to raise any objections.

The bearers stopped and lowered the palanquin to the ground. It appeared they had reached Oen's house in Shinmeichô.

"We're here!" the men shouted loudly enough to be heard inside the house. But no one came out to greet Oen. She handed the bearers their tip and rushed up to the front door.

"Ofuyu!" Her voice seemed to echo clear through to the back of the house. She then called the maid's name but got the same response.

Oen entered the house and stepped from the hallway into the sitting room. The four-and-a-half-mat room was as tidy as it had been the day before yesterday when Oen had left the house. But the door of the closet in the three-mat room next door had been left open, and inside Oen saw an empty trunk. It belonged to Otake, the maid.

Oen raced upstairs, afraid that the house had been burgled. But on the second floor she found nothing out of place. Her everyday kimono still hung on the clothes rack, wrinkles and all.

Oen heard the sound of voices; it seemed to come from the alleyway behind the house. Stepping outside onto the balcony used for hanging out laundry, Oen almost tripped over a wooden bucket. It contained some clothes that had been washed and wrung out but were still waiting to be hung up. Not only that, but one end of the clothes pole was resting on the floor, blocking Oen's path. Clicking her tongue in annoyance, she picked up the end of the pole and put it back in place, then leaned over the balcony's railing.

Ofuyu was below in the alleyway, talking to her young samurai. Oen was just wondering whether to call out to her when Ofuyu, apparently becoming aware she was being watched, looked up and saw Oen, whereupon she threw up her hands and rushed back into the house. Not in the least perturbed, the young man also looked up and bowed politely at Oen before walking off down the alleyway.

Oen dashed downstairs. Ofuyu had just carried the small clay brazier into the alley and was in the process of lighting it, intending to boil water for tea.

"I'm sorry," she said when she heard Oen's footsteps behind her, "but Otake has run off and I've had a million things to do." Her back was still turned away from Oen.

"Chatting with your boyfriend being among them, I suppose," Oen said teasingly. Pretending not to have heard, Ofuyu began fanning the brazier. "Well, never mind that. Why has Otake gone off?"

"She said her older sister in Zôshigaya has died," replied Ofuyu, turning to look at Oen. "One of her neighbors—a Mrs. Something-or-other—came by a little while ago to fetch her."

"My, she must have been in a state."

"Yes. Her sister's husband died three years ago, she said, so now she'll have to look after her niece and her nephew. She ran out of the house without even taking time to pack a few things. She said she'd be back later, though."

But even if Otake were to return, she could hardly continue as Oen's maid with a young niece and nephew to look after.

"Actually . . ." Ofuyu began, untying the sash that held back the sleeves of her kimono and standing up. The brazier was lit and an iron kettle sat over the flame. "There's a favor I've been wanting to ask you, but now that Otake's gone it makes it kind of awkward."

"What is it?"

Was Ofuyu going to announce she was leaving as well? Oen wondered. She quickly dismissed the thought. Ofuyu's relationship with the *hatamoto*'s son had gone on for three years, but serious as that might seem, there was no way a penniless younger son like Kishimoto would ever marry a girl like Ofuyu. Unless he found a family without any sons willing to adopt him, or otherwise demonstrated an exceptional ability for affairs of state, a samurai in his position would have to forgo marriage altogether. And yet Ofuyu, stumbling slightly over the words, said the last thing Ofuyu had expected to hear.

"What's that? You're getting married?"

"Yes, everything has worked out. He's been adopted by the Surugaya."

"The Surugaya—you mean that saké business?"

Ofuyu looked at Oen and nodded. The owner of the Surugaya was one of Oen's biggest fans. She had never been invited to perform for him in private, but whenever she appeared on stage he would have a large casket of saké delivered to her dressing room.

Oen recalled having once ordered some folding fans with her name on them to give to her most loyal supporters. Thinking back on it now, she had sent Ofuyu round to the Surugaya to deliver one. That must have been how Ofuyu had gotten to know the owner.

"I'm sorry for keeping all this from you," Ofuyu said.

Oen looked away.

"It happened this past spring. I went round to see the owner of the Surugaya to ask his advice about what I should do, and he said that since he didn't have any children he would adopt him—just like that!"

"Really?"

"I'm sorry, Miss Oshichi." Ofuyu bowed deeply, putting her hands on the floor. "I'd like to leave as soon as possible, if that's all right with you. You see, I'm going to have a child."

"Is that so?" Oen turned her back on Ofuyu. "Here, I return in a good mood, and what do I find? Everyone's leaving!" she complained.

"Please, miss."

"All right. But hang out the laundry in the bucket upstairs first!"

Oen went into the sitting room and shut the door.

⁓

The Momozonotei had decided to promote Oen to *shinkatari* starting from September. The theater's owner, Manbei, showed her the hand-written agenda he had sent the other theater owners with her name in the top slot. Leading off the show as *habakatari* would be another of Senjo's protégées, a girl younger than Kosen. Oen thanked Manbei and handed the piece of paper back to him.

"Aren't you pleased?" he asked, knocking his pipe against the side of the ash bucket. He seemed surprised that Oen wasn't jumping for joy or purring coquettishly at his feet.

"I'm so happy it's left me feeling somewhat numb," she replied. In truth, she herself was surprised at how subdued her feelings were.

Why, when I've wanted this for so long? she wondered to herself.

The other day, Chôemon had come to tell Oen he had sent a kimono round to Senjo on her behalf. Also, Kusutarô told her that according to his *hatamoto* friend, Senjo had said she expected Oen to make a bigger name for herself than Kosen. Oen had made a show of being overjoyed by this news, but in fact she wasn't all that excited.

Oen walked home from the Momozonotei. The wind on the back of her neck made it feel as though it were already autumn.

As she slid open the latticed front door, a fifty-something woman poked her head out. It was the retired lady next door whom Oen had asked to keep an eye on things while she was out. After the woman had gone home, Oen was alone in the house. It had been like that for the past five days. The first maid she had hired to replace Otake had turned out to have sticky fingers, and the next one had been downright lazy.

Two girls had recently come to learn *jôruri* from Oen. They seemed to be under the misapprehension, however, that becoming students of the most popular singer of the day would immediately open doors for them. They left as soon as they realized Oen's influence wasn't enough to get them onto the stage—one had lasted just three days, the other two weeks.

Oen sat down in front of the large charcoal brazier in the living room to have some tea. Just then she remembered that before going out she had left some clothes hanging out to dry on the upstairs balcony.

It was getting close to sunset. There wasn't much charcoal in the house and Oen wanted to go to the bathhouse before preparing dinner. Once again, it looked as though she wouldn't have time for her usual afternoon cup of tea. What's more, rehearsal would have to wait until first thing in the morning. Oen's legs felt strangely tired as she dragged herself up the stairs.

The other day Ofuyu and her new husband had dropped by to say hello. Ofuyu's pregnancy had started to show and she thrust her stomach forward as she walked. Her former samurai husband—whose commoner hairstyle suited him very nicely—had been very attentive to Ofuyu throughout their visit, taking her hand as she stepped down from the hall into the entranceway on their way out so that she wouldn't fall.

"That's the last kind of man I need," Oen muttered to herself as she held the laundry in her arms.

What a young *jôruri* singer such as herself needed were steady patrons she could rely on. She was only interested in scions of samurai families with large annual incomes who were willing to actually pay for her company. Less well-heeled samurai would spring for a cheap ticket at a vaudeville theater to see her perform once or twice a month and offer to escort her home, but they were no good to her at all when she needed some extra cash. Even worse were the second and third sons of samurai families, who were as likely as not to end up burdens to their elder brothers. Such fans were totally worthless to her.

And yet Ofuyu had persisted in loving one such a worthless man. Their love had only been possible because Ofuyu had never shown one iota of improvement as a singer. It was because she preferred cooking stewed potatoes and doing laundry to rehearsing that Ofuyu had been happy to settle for such a worthless man.

"Not me . . ." muttered Oen. *I could never do that.*

The cold never bothered Oen during her early morning rehearsals on the balcony in the dead of winter, but stepping outside to wash clothes and feeling the frost under her feet was more than she could bear. Many a time she had sat plucking away at her samisen, hunger gnawing away inside her simply because she didn't want to waste time preparing something to eat.

Oen recalled how she had waited impatiently to hear from Kusutarô and then gone to meet him at the teahouse in Ueno. Yet as soon as they had finished making love she had immediately felt the urge to go back to rehearsing. She thought of how she had accepted Chôemon's help while falling in love with Kusutarô. How she had thrown herself into Chôemon's arms while thinking longingly of Kusutarô. Hadn't she done all this because the only thing she really cared about was her music?

Oen took from these two men what was necessary for her music: money and her sensuality. Was it any surprise that Chôemon should develop an attraction to his copyist? Was it any wonder that Kusutarô should hesitate to go directly to the *hatamoto*'s house to intercede on her behalf?

But in fact, Oen had been relieved to hear that the copyist, Hasegawa Rikô, had rebuffed Chôemon's advances. Likewise, there were times when she truly yearned to be with Kusutarô. Even so, she didn't think she could devote herself to one man as Ofuyu did.

Oen took money but had nothing left over for herself. She delivered impassioned performances but then she went home to a lifeless, empty house. Ofuyu, on the other hand, had found a samurai willing to throw aside his sword for her. A man who held his hand out to his pregnant wife so she wouldn't fall. A husband whom she could count on to return home, unlike Chôemon and Kusutarô, who went home to their own houses after making love to Oen.

What's so great about being a star?

Noticing she was crying, Oen wiped her tears away with the clean clothes she had just brought inside. She had no time for tears. She had run out of lamp oil and charcoal. She had to go to the grocer's and the bathhouse. After dinner, if possible, she wanted to run through *The Saké Shop* one more time.

Oen put her coin purse into the breast of her kimono and stepped out the front door. First she went to the oil dealer's, filled her container, brought it home, and left it in the hallway inside the front door. Then she headed off to the charcoal shop. On the way home, as she approached her house, she heard someone call out her stage name. She turned to see a face covered with pimples, wearing a smile that looked like it was glued on.

"What luck running into you like this, Miss Shichinosuke," he said, loudly enough to make people in the street turn and stare. "Even though I escorted you home that time I couldn't remember where your house was. I've been looking all over for it!"

Matajûrô blushed under Oen's gaze and scratched the back of his neck in embarrassment. "I, um, thought it'd be nice to see you sometime, and since you're always so busy, I decided to come see *you* instead."

Fool, halfwit, numbskull, moron! In her mind, Oen heaped every form of abuse she could think of onto the unsuspecting Matajûrô. *Don't you get it? I'm busy because I don't want to see you!*

Oblivious, Matajûrô bowed deeply from the waist. "Thank you. I wanted to express my most sincere gratitude for what you have done." Not knowing what on earth he had to thank *her* for, Oen only stared silently at the young samurai. At last, Matajûrô straightened up. He looked relieved to have gotten what he had come to say off his chest. "I'm so glad I came to Edo!" he gushed.

"But I don't know why you're thanking me," responded Oen.

"You've treated me to the most sublime *jôruri* I've ever heard."

Oen said nothing. Apparently misconstruing her silence to mean she hadn't heard him, Matajûrô repeated himself—only much more loudly this time.

"Would you like to stop in for a moment?" Oen suddenly blurted out, taking even herself by surprise. Matajûrô turned bright crimson. The mere mention of entering her house was enough to make him blush. "Please. It's no trouble at all."

"No, really, all I came to do was express my gratitude."

"But I can't turn away so ardent an admirer of my work just like that." Oen opened the front door and stood waiting for Matajûrô. Stepping over the threshold, he turned an even darker shade of crimson. "Please come into the sitting room."

"Really, I'll be fine right here. In fact, I prefer to be here," he said, sitting down on the step inside the front door. He rested his clenched fists on his knees, looking as though not even wild horses would get him to budge.

Oen did not insist. She carried the sack of charcoal into the kitchen. Matajûrô seemed to relax now that he could no longer see her face. She heard his voice from the hall.

"You were abandoned as a child, I hear." Oen, who was preparing tea, gave a wry smile. It seemed this particular subject always came up in connection with her. "My cousin told me about it that time we met you at the restaurant in Negishi."

"It's quite embarrassing, really."

"There's nothing to be embarrassed about. I nearly flew off the handle and drew my sword until I heard that."

"Oh, my. Had I made some sort of blunder?" Oen put a bowl of sweet bean jelly and a pair of teacups on a tray and carried it out to the hall where Matajûrô was seated.

He blinked at her as though looking into a bright light. "Heavens! You couldn't do any such thing. No, what enraged me was seeing all the food being served to us when back home there are samurai who don't even have millet to eat. I couldn't believe how self-indulgent Edo people are."

Oen placed a cup of tea in front of Matajûrô and said nothing. She was tempted to reply that that was probably why, up until now, she had always found samurai from the provinces so unpleasant.

"But then my cousin said that despite being abandoned as a child you'd become the biggest celebrity in Edo, and it took ages to book you for a private party like that. I tell you, I was dumbstruck. You must be an amazing person to have become such a big star, but Edo people must be amazing, too, to have allowed you to succeed."

"I was just lucky, I guess."

Matajûrô picked up his cup and sipped his tea. "I was born into a samurai house with an income of seven hundred bushels of rice," he continued, "but I was the fifth son. So I was adopted by another family, one with an income of just thirty bales."

Thirty bales! Oen now understood why Matajûrô had been angered rather than impressed by the food served at the restaurant in Negishi.

"Once a family with thirty bales, always a family with thirty bales. My son will have just thirty bales, and *his* son will have just thirty bales. At present we've got just barely enough to eat, but what will happen if prices rise any higher? No one can give me an answer. I feel like the world has abandoned us."

"How do you mean abandoned . . . ?"

"Once I came to Edo I understood. It wasn't only us poor provincial samurai who've been abandoned; shogunal retainers with incomes of seventy bales, *hatamoto* with two hundred—we're all in the same boat. Generation after generation, we're condemned to live in poverty. Those samurai don't flock to see you because seats at the vaudeville theaters are cheap. They come because they want to succeed in the world on their own merits, like you have."

"Forgive me. I don't understand such complicated matters."

"That's okay—you don't need to understand. Just hurry up and become *shinkatari*." Matajûrô sipped what was left of his tea.

A hush fell over the house and Oen heard a woman's voice outside. It was the hairdresser across the street stopping a book lender to ask unsuccessfully if she could borrow something by Ryûtei Tanehiko, whose novels were all the rage in Edo at the moment.

"Well, actually . . ." Oen began hesitantly. "From September, I'll be the *shinkatari* at the Momozonotei."

"That's wonderful!" A smile spread across Matajûrô's pimply face and his beady eyes narrowed until they were barely more than slits. "Now I feel like I'm moving up in the world, too!" he added.

I'm glad to hear that, Oen thought. At that moment, she was glad everything had turned out the way it had. That she had been abandoned as a child. That she had been taken in by a *jôruri* teacher. That she had not simply married one of her fans.

"That's something to look forward to, then," Matajûrô said. He stood up, said goodbye to her in his formal manner, and, without so much as waiting for her to step down from the hallway, slid open the lattice door and left.

She rushed out into the street after him. Matajûrô was already walking quickly away down Oen's tiny street, bathed in the evening glow. After some distance he stopped and looked back, perhaps sensing that Oen was watching. She gave a deep bow. During their conversation, she had given Matajûrô her undivided attention. Her mind had not been focused on *jôruri,* as it always was when speaking to Chôemon or Kusutarô.

Probably her relationship with Matajûrô would never go any further. Probably—much as she wanted to give Chôemon and Kusutarô her undivided attention without always thinking about *jôruri*—she would continue speaking to them as though her back was turned. But supposing she had a sudden urge to see their faces and turned to look at them—what would she see? Probably she would find that their backs were turned to her as well.

That's all right, I don't mind, she thought to herself.

Spotting Oen outside her house, the boy who lived across the street rushed up to her. As he held out his hand, she saw he was holding a white piece of paper. Oen handed the child a coin and opened the note, which had been folded in three. It was a message from Kusutarô. He was at a restaurant near the Shinmei Shrine and would stop by to see her on his way home.

Regretting she hadn't cleaned the house, Oen decided she would rehearse *The Saké Shop* until Kusutarô arrived.

IV

~ INNOCENT IN LOVE ~

Okon opened her eyes.

Not yet fully awake, she was unsure at first where she was. When she came to her senses after a moment, she realized she was lying on the futon where she always slept, in the middle of a ten-mat tatami room that was unnecessarily large for one person.

With a rueful smile, Okon turned over in bed. She had been dreaming she was making love to a man whose face she couldn't quite make out, and his touch remained with her even now that she was awake. Widely considered by those who knew her to be indifferent to men, Okon felt that her dream had revealed something deep within her being that she herself had long ignored.

She threw aside her pillow and turned onto her stomach. The night was drawing to a close. Faint beams of light filtered through the gaps in the rain shutters enclosing the veranda, illuminating the room's newly repapered shoji in a white glow.

Despite a sense of weariness Okon knew she had to get out of bed. She needed to get straight to work on something that had been troubling her for the past few days: the design for a new ornamental hairpin. She sat up in bed and reached for the kimono hanging on her clothes rack.

Okon's shop was a venerable boutique called the Sasaya that had built a reputation on selling fashionable and exquisitely crafted hairpins. And for customers who preferred to place special orders, the

Sasaya was known for its ability to meet and surpass even the most demanding expectations. The hairpins on sale in the Sasaya were supplied by a trusted silversmith whom Okon's family had relied on for years.

But for some time Okon had been frustrated by the fact that her family's business sold only goods that attracted a well-heeled clientele. The Sasaya had made its name as a purveyor of luxury goods back in her great-grandfather's day, and though she wouldn't go so far as to say he had been mistaken, Okon believed it to be an overly conservative business model. Rather than being known for selling upscale merchandise, she would have preferred to put the Sasaya's hairpins on the heads of women all over Edo.

Okon had come up with her first original hairpin design five years ago—the same year in which she had lost first her father and then her elder brother—with an ornament featuring a pair of mandarin ducks. Containing less silver and priced more affordably than the Sasaya's usual offerings, Okon's duck hairpins had proven a great success and sales had exceeded even her own wildest expectations.

Ever since, she had offered in her shop a line of affordably priced hairpins designed personally by her, sold under the label "The Okon Collection." Last spring she had created one featuring a rapeseed blossom ornament with tiny dangling silver chains, reviving a fashion popular many years before. It too had sold extremely well. It was said that one couldn't turn a corner without seeing some young woman wearing one of Okon's hairpins. While perhaps it could not yet be said that the Sasaya's hairpins graced coiffures throughout Edo, they had at any rate won Okon quite a following.

But the hairpin she had designed this past autumn as a tie-in to a hit kabuki play running at the Nakamuraza theater had been a complete flop. The play, *Love Letter from the Licensed Quarter,* had opened in October as the highlight of the Nakamuraza's daily performance schedule. The roles of the courtesan Yûgiri and her lover Izaemon were played by Bandô Mitsugorô and Nakamura Shikan, who exchanged roles every other day. Garnering rave reviews, it was playing to packed houses day in and day out.

When Okon had learned that this particular play was scheduled to open at the Nakamuraza, she had decided to create a new hairpin design, again using silver chains. The continued popularity of her rapeseed blossom hairpin had reconfirmed her belief that the once-popular fashion still had life in it yet. What's more, there was no denying that the silver chains were very attractive dangling down over a young girl's forehead.

This time, Okon's idea had been to use longer, narrower chains to evoke wisps of mist, an allusion to the name of the play's heroine, Yûgiri, or "Evening Mist." The hairpin was adorned with a love letter folded accordion-style as in the play. She had expected it to be hailed another brilliant success for the Sasaya, with young women shoving each other aside in their haste to purchase one.

To top it all off, Okon had arranged for lines to be inserted into the actors' dialogue touting her hairpins, and she'd even asked a *gesaku* writer to make up some advertising fliers. Given all this, she would not have been surprised if customers had flooded into the Sasaya the moment she opened her doors for business.

Yet despite her best efforts, the hairpins had been a failure. A young female *jôruri* singer named Shichinosuke, having seen the play and heard Okon's hairpins advertised, came to the Sasaya with one of her admirers intending to have him buy her one, but they left without making a purchase. "No, this won't do at all," Okon heard her say with complete candor.

As she finished tying the sash of her kimono, Okon pressed her fingers against her temples. Her Yûgiri hairpin's poor showing had even started to hurt sales of her once popular duck and rapeseed blossom designs, making her that much more determined to put out another new design first thing in the spring. Yesterday, however, her head clerk had expressed his opinion that the Sasaya ought to return to the sound business principles of the past. Inexpensive merchandise had a short shelf life—if indeed it sold at all, he told her.

But Okon was unwilling to abandon her dream of putting her hairpins on women all over Edo. If her next design proved a success it would pull up sales of her Yûgiri hairpin along with it. To get people's attention, she would have to come up with something both visually appealing and not too expensive, but as yet she had no idea what that might be.

Still massaging her temples, Okon walked out of her room into the corridor.

_‿◦◦‿_

A cold wind whipped past Okon and she came to a sudden stop.

She had gone to a fabric shop in Owarichô to get her mind off work for a while. Having ordered some kimono material to be dyed with a pattern of small hairpins, she was now on her way home.

One moment it was sweltering, then, before I knew it, autumn had arrived. Now winter . . . Last night, she had drawn the charcoal brazier close to her, trying without success to warm her knees as she sat pondering her new hairpin design. The weather's turning cold, Okon thought; time to get out the kotatsu table and quilt. Soon it might even snow.

Snow . . .

A bolt of lightning flashed in her head.

That's it—a pine tree covered in snow!

Silver pine needles covered in silver snow—the concept was a bit plain, but it just might work. These days sixteen- and seventeen-year-old girls preferred an elegant, mature look that belied their years.

I'll give it a try.

Hardly able to contain her excitement, Okon set off home at a run. Her surprised maid called out for her to wait but Okon pretended not to hear.

The Sasaya was located on the corner of the first block of Okechô. Okon was in too much of a hurry to go around to the back door and rushed straight in through the entrance to the shop.

"Look out!"

Okon saw the tall man coming out of the shop but was unable to stop herself in time. She ran into him and would have been sent flying if he hadn't reached out and held her to him. His chest was strong and muscular. Blushing furiously, Okon stepped away and, avoiding looking at his face, uttered a few words of apology.

"Not at all," he replied. "I wasn't paying attention either."

The voice sounded familiar. Timidly, Okon raised her head to see a pair of long, narrow eyes with a twinkle in them.

"It's been a while," he said.

"Why, it's you!"

His name was Hidesaburô and he was the third son of a soy sauce dealer. Six years ago he had married into a family that owned a candle shop in Okechô. Okon blushed again, embarrassed to be seen in such a state by her former childhood playmate.

"What a surprise. I didn't think *anything* made you blush, Okon!"

"What mean things you say!" Okon put her hands to her cheeks and glared at Hidesaburô. "I see you're as sarcastic as ever. How long is it since I last saw you—about two years?"

"Don't you remember? I ran into you late last year over there on that corner. I guess you've been so engrossed in your work you've already forgotten."

Okon gave a rather shrill laugh. "Let's not stand here talking— come in and have some tea, won't you?"

"I'm afraid I can't right now." Hidesaburô suddenly glanced anxiously toward the steady stream of people passing by in the street as though he were in a hurry. "I've been to see my elder brother about something and I just thought I'd pop in here on my way home. I was interested to see what kind of hairpins you were making these days."

"Yes, speaking of which . . ." Okon faltered. It wasn't that she minded telling Hidesaburô her new design was not selling as well as she had hoped, but she didn't want to admit to him that it was a complete flop.

"So is it true the singer Shichinosuke came to your shop?"

"Uh-huh," Okon replied vaguely, nodding her head. She wondered how much Hidesaburô had heard about her new hairpins.

As a child, Okon had attended the same primary school as Hidesaburô. The boys were taught writing, arithmetic and, if they wished, studied old scholarly Chinese texts such as *The Four Books and Five Classics* and *The Selection of Epistolary Writings*. The girls studied only Japanese textbooks like *Education for Women* and *Elementary Letter Writing,* in addition to needlework and tea ceremony. Despite her different schooling, Okon had managed to memorize Confucius' *Analects* merely by listening to the boys recite it as she sat nearby sewing. The other children had taken to calling her "the new Murasaki" after the great

Murasaki Shikibu, author of *The Tale of Genji,* who was said to have memorized her elder brother's lessons faster than him simply by listening to him read them aloud.

It had evidently vexed Hidesaburô to be shown up in this way by a girl three years his junior. He had taken it as a challenge and set about memorizing all the teachings of Confucius and Mencius at such a blistering pace that Okon was unable to keep up. This time it was Okon's turn to be vexed. She envied Hidesaburô for being able to ask the teacher every time he came across a word he didn't understand, and she chaffed at having to sit nearby sewing dolls' kimonos.

Hidesaburô had gone on to marry the daughter of the owner of the Tatsumiya candle shop, and just three years later—that is, two years ago—a bizarre trend had become all the rage in Edo. If a girl had a crush on some boy, she would buy a candle with her name carved on it and place it, without his knowing, into the lantern he carried with him. When he lit the candle, it was believed, a spell would be cast on him that would cause him to fall in love with her. In fact, it was Hidesaburô who had dreamed up this innocent little game.

Having heard so much about these magic candles, Okon finally decided she had to see for herself what it was all about. So she went to Okechô and stood in line at the Tatsumiya with a bunch of mothers and nannies who were presumably there at the behest of their daughters. After making her purchase she was handed what appeared to be nothing more than a perfectly ordinary candle, except that near the top, barely more than a scratch, was her name. She had had to admire Hidesaburô's sheer brilliance at being able to get people to wait in line with so little effort on his part.

The next day, Hidesaburô had come to see Okon. It seemed that someone who worked at his shop had told him the proprietress of the Sasaya had been in to buy a candle.

"Actually," Hidesaburô said as soon as he saw her, "it was your hairpins that gave me the idea." Apparently he assumed from the very beginning that Okon had not bought the candle because she had a crush on someone.

"I knew it!" responded Okon with a smile.

Okon was aware Hidesaburô bought one of her hairpins whenever she came out with a new design. Her clerk and his assistant always joked about it, saying an adopted son-in-law had to make sure to keep his wife happy, but Okon suspected there was more to it than that. Ever since they had been in school together, Hidesaburô had not paid much attention to anyone but Okon.

"Some people think it's enough to run the shop the way it's always been run, the customers be damned," he had told her, "but when I saw your hairpins, I realized there's more than one way to sell candles too." The Tatsumiya had been doing brisk business ever since. If there was one person Okon didn't want to know about her disastrous new hairpin, it was Hidesaburô.

"This one's not bad either, actually." Hidesaburô reached into the breast of his kimono and took out a handkerchief folded in two. Inside was Okon's Yûgiri hairpin. "I have to confess, I have a new idea for a candle I want to sell, but my father-in-law is against it. That's what I went to talk to my brother about just now, but he also advised me to forget about it. I thought it might cheer me up to drop by and look at your hairpins."

"Really?" Okon was inclined to suspect Hidesaburô knew just how unpopular her new design was and was taking consolation in the thought that even Okon put a foot wrong from time to time.

"By the way," began Hidesaburô, changing the subject. He seemed to have forgotten that he was in a hurry. "Have you seen Heita lately?"

Heita was another former classmate of theirs, the son of a tobacconist just off the main street. He had been Hidesaburô's polar opposite—a little ruffian who nicked toys and candies from shops and distributed them among children he referred to as his "boys." He was always getting into trouble at school, being beaten by the teacher or made to stand in the corner. Once he'd taken his rage out on Okon, the teacher's pet, by hurling a dead mouse at her.

"I've only seen him two or three times since he moved to Shin-Ôsakachô," Okon replied.

"He's running his own business now."

"A business?"

"Didn't you know? Heita's father bought a cotton merchant's license." Hidesaburô folded the hairpin back up in his handkerchief. "Well, I suppose I best be going," he said. "Sorry to have stood here talking your ear off."

As Hidesaburô shoved his handkerchief back into the breast of his kimono, Okon thought of asking him to stay a bit longer, but then she suddenly remembered the idea she had had for her new hairpin. For the sake of appearances, she stood there for a moment and watched him go before darting into her shop.

Okon passed two sleepless nights working on her new design, but when she showed it to the Sasaya's silversmith and head clerk they both merely frowned. The silversmith, for his part, said the intricate detail the pine needles called for was a welcome challenge, but for that amount of effort he preferred she price it with the more expensive merchandise. The head clerk dismissed the whole design out of hand, saying he saw nothing particularly appealing about a snow-covered pine tree.

Okon wadded her designs into a ball and hurled them at the waste-paper basket. She had just overheard the head clerk speaking to his assistant, and his words still rang in her ears. "She's got a good head on her shoulders, but when it comes right down to it, she's a woman," he had said, not aware that Okon was listening. "When the merchandise isn't selling, women don't have the business acumen to step back and reevaluate what it is their customers really want."

Indeed! Well, who gives you that fat vacation allowance every year, then? she shot back, though only in her head. *And if the customers aren't buying my merchandise, how is it we can afford to hire that expensive silversmith we couldn't before?*

Despite the fact that business was booming, the head clerk wanted to stick Okon's designer hairpins away into a corner of the shop. And even though Okon promised him a good wage, the silversmith pre-ferred to do one-off made-to-order items. One man balked at sell-ing low-end merchandise, the other said it was a waste of his talent. Okon wondered what they would have said if instead of her, it had been her father or her elder brother who had come up with the idea for The Okon Collection? Wouldn't the head clerk have agreed the Sasaya could not continue to sell only high-end merchandise? Wouldn't the silversmith have conceded he wanted his skill to become known throughout Edo? It seemed to Okon that they spurned her ideas and treated her the way they did simply because she was a woman.

She finished her tea, which had become tepid, and went out into the shop. There were no customers. The Sasaya's assistant clerk and errand boy were sitting around looking bored. It sounded as though there was a visitor upstairs in the room above the shop—probably that retired gentleman who lives over in Kuramae, thought Okon. He had been coming to the Sasaya since her grandfather's day to order fancy custom-made hairpins for his various mistresses. But recently even he had taken to saying he no longer felt like patronizing the Sasaya on account of the cheap line of hairpins Okon was selling these days.

Feeling as though she were in hostile territory, Okon left the shop. The late autumn sun shone on the Sasaya's weathered signboard. She recalled how she had run into Hidesaburô on this very spot. If anyone seemed to have the wind at his back it was Hidesaburô—people were always saying how lucky the Tatsumiya's owner was to have found such a good son-in law. And yet according to Hidesaburô, even *he* was facing stiff opposition from his father-in-law—his own brother even—over some new candles he wanted to sell.

Okon decided to head over to Okechô and look in on him. From what she had heard, Hidesaburô's magic candles were no longer the best-selling items they once were, so he probably would have time to chat with her for a while.

Perhaps, she thought, she ought to change into a better kimono before heading over. She started to turn back but then remembered the head clerk sitting behind the lattice partition at the back of the shop going over the accounts on his abacus, and the thought of seeing his face filled her with dread. Plus there was no reason for her to get all dressed up just to go see an old schoolmate—a married man with a wife and child, no less—to talk about mundane business matters.

Okon walked along Okechô's main street, passing its many sober bookshops selling religious tracts and history texts, until she reached the third corner where she turned down a side street. Here the crowds thinned out somewhat. She continued to the next corner, on which stood the Tatsumiya. The side gate had been left open and next to it a cart was leaning against the fence. It appeared a delivery of goods had just been unloaded.

Hidesaburô was probably busy inspecting the new delivery, Okon thought as she entered the shop. Just then, he emerged from the back of the shop. When he saw Okon he clapped his hands together in surprise and burst into laughter exclaiming, "You've come at just the right time!"

Okon tilted her head questioningly.

"Hei'emon is here—from the Kuzu'uya," he added.

"Hei'emon . . . the Kuzu'uya?" queried Okon. The names meant nothing to her.

Handing the account ledger he was holding in his hand to his head clerk, Hidesaburô beckoned Okon over to him. "You remember . . . we were just talking about him the other day. Heita—the tobacconist's son. Heita is now Hei'emon, master of the Kuzu'uya. Let's go in that way," he motioned, explaining that the veranda overlooking the garden at back was full of laborers sitting around drinking saké, while the sitting room was occupied by his father-in-law, who was discussing business with a retailer.

They passed through a curtain hanging halfway to the ground at the back of the shop, which led to a small two-mat room that appeared to be used for storage. Beyond that lay another two-mat room. To the right was the front door to the main part of the house, and to the left was apparently the drawing room.

As they walked through the rooms, Hidesaburô told Okon how Heita's father had over the years managed to save up enough money to buy his cotton business by collecting scrap paper and turning it into notebooks, which he sold. As a boy, Heita had always worn cast-off straw sandals his father picked up in the street.

Leaving the second of the two rooms, they emerged into an L-shaped passageway. Opposite them was a pair of shoji. Hidesaburô slid them open and they entered what appeared to be a living room used by Hidesaburô and his wife.

Sitting with his back to the small alcove in the corner of the room was a swarthy man who wore a determined look. He was surprisingly well built for the son of a prosperous cotton merchant. Over his sturdy frame he wore a blue-and-white-striped kimono that suited him admirably.

"Heita, is that really you?" Okon asked somewhat tentatively. Surely this was not the same boy that had lived on the street behind hers, she thought to herself.

"Okon?" The man's look of determination broke into a broad smile, and in his eyes Okon recognized the boy she remembered from her childhood.

Okon sat down across from him. "It's been ages, hasn't it? How many years is it since we last saw each other, I wonder?" she asked.

"Let's see now—I saw you two or three times after I moved, but that must be eighteen or nineteen years ago now."

So it was, Okon thought. At that time, Heita had still been wearing threadbare clothes and muddy straw sandals that dragged on the ground as he walked. "Now I wouldn't recognize you even if I ran into you on the street!" she exclaimed.

"But I'd recognize you!" he shot back. He sounded, anyway, like the same old Heita.

Hidesaburô's wife entered the room bearing a tray of tea and cakes. Her name was Ochie. After greeting them in a tiny whisper of a voice—like the buzzing of a mosquito, thought Okon—she immediately withdrew from the room. Perhaps being an only child, she had been coddled and protected, Okon mused.

"She seems like a good wife—very demure," Heita said.

"Looks can be deceiving," replied Hidesaburô, smiling, as he returned to the room after stepping outside to grab his wife and ask her to bring them some saké.

"My old lady's a real cheerful one—that's good, of course, except that she never shuts up."

"Oito—isn't that her name? How old are your children now?"

"Four and three. And yours?"

"We just had our first one last year."

Okon sat silently watching the faces of the two men as they talked about their children. Heita looked at Okon. He seemed to want to bring her into the conversation but was having trouble thinking of something to talk about.

In the end, it was Okon who put a question to him. "Are you parents both well, Heita?" she asked.

"My mother died ten years ago. My old man passed away just last year."

"What? I had no idea!" exclaimed Hidesaburô.

"Yeah, the damned fool—there he scrimped and saved all those years, and just when our business really took off he went and kicked the bucket."

"I'm sure your parents looking down from heaven are very proud of what you've made of yourself," said Okon.

"I understand you also lost your father and your older brother, Okon."

"Yes."

"Even so, I never thought to find you still single," Heita said, blinking as though a light had been shined in his eyes. "Didn't you have a fiancé at some point?"

"Yes, well, that didn't quite work out," replied Okon, her voice raspy. "Talk about being a damn fool—it turned out he had a lover!"

She explained that her father had been incensed when he had found out and had gone and broken off the engagement. "And there I was about to give him my precious daughter!" he had exclaimed. Okon had been sixteen. It seemed her father had been approached with several other proposals after that but for one reason or another none had passed muster with him. Then he had died and within the year, she lost her brother as well.

Even now, Okon was proud of how she had managed to pull the Sasaya through the traumatic period following the death of two proprietors in quick succession. When her uncle-cum-guardian had come to propose she marry his own son so he could take over the business, she had politely declined. Instead, she had decided to follow through on her plan to launch The Okon Collection, which her brother had agreed to before his death. The head clerk and other employees had been set against it but her uncle had convinced them to drop their opposition, no doubt calculating that when Okon's plan failed she would come running back to him for help.

But her plan had not failed. Her duck hairpins had flown off the shelves. "It just goes to show what times we live in that something like this will sell," scoffed the head clerk and the other employees, though without going so far as to admit they'd been wrong. Still, when her uncle interfered too much they did Okon the favor of looking displeased and asking him to keep his opinions to himself.

From then on, Okon had thrown herself into running the business, in close consultation with the head clerk. Though the number of marriage proposals she received had dropped after The Okon Collection became popular, this was offset by an increase in the number of men making passes at her. But knowing they merely regarded her as a plaything, Okon was not much interested in getting involved in romance. Once, half on a lark, she had even taken a love letter she'd received and gone round to the man's house to return it.

"Now I'm simply enjoying my work too much to think about marriage," said Okon, concluding her story.

"You always were very clever, Okon," responded Heita with obvious admiration. A faint smile rose to Hidesaburô's lips. From the other side of the shoji, Okon heard what sounded like the faint buzzing of a mosquito, and a moment later Ochie came in with a tray of saké.

⁓

It seemed as though only a moment ago the bell outside had sounded four o'clock but now it was already growing dark. Okon had been working all afternoon on her pine tree design and had at last made some good progress. She shunted her desk closer to the shoji and opened them, trying to let in more light.

Just then her maid, Omaki, poked her head into the room. Hidesaburô was here to see her, she said. On the verge of finishing her work for the day, Okon couldn't be bothered to get up and go into the sitting room, so she told Omaki to show him in.

Omaki returned shortly with the candle maker, who seemed taken aback by the sheer size of Okon's desk, which was blocking the entrance to the room, and by the papers strewn all over it. Okon asked him to wait a moment and Hidesaburô nodded and sat down in the corridor.

"Working on a new design?" he asked, craning his neck to look at the papers lying on the desk.

"Yes—what do you think of it?" Okon asked, laying down her brush.

Hidesaburô picked up one of the drawings, blowing vigorously over the paper where the ink was not completely dry. Okon half expected to hear him exclaim, "Splendid, Okon!" or something to that effect. Instead he merely laid the drawing back down on the desk without saying a word.

"I've captured the pine tree in an interesting way, don't you think?" she asked him.

Hidesaburô's only response was: "How about getting something to eat?" Okon stared at him. It was as though he had told her he didn't think much of her design. "C'mon, it doesn't hurt to treat yourself once in a while," Hidesaburô said, standing up and gazing out at the darkness that was beginning to engulf the garden. "I'm still upset with my father-in-law for rejecting my idea to make candles in the shapes of the twelve animals of the Chinese zodiac. I thought they would be popular for parties and such, but he said candles should look like candles. That was the end of that . . . I'll be waiting for you at the Yoshizawa restaurant in Muromachi."

Hidesaburô glanced over his shoulder at Okon. She noticed that even the famously handsome Hidesaburô was starting to get wrinkles on his forehead, and that under his eyes there were shadows that seemed to indicate he wasn't getting enough sleep.

—⚬⚬—

Okon straightened up her room herself and took her time changing into another kimono. The bell sounded six o'clock just as she was leaving the house. In the shop, the clerks had already brought down the front shutters and were hard at work adding up sums on their abacuses.

Hidesaburô must have told the Yoshizawa's proprietress he was expecting Okon, for as soon as she parted the curtain at the entrance to the restaurant and stepped inside, the woman motioned her upstairs.

Despite the chill in the air outside, Hidesaburô was seated by the open window looking out at the stars that had begun twinkling in the sky. At his feet lay a tray containing a saké pot and a cup. It appeared that he had already polished off a round all by himself.

A waitress immediately arrived with their meal. Hidesaburô closed the window and picked up the fresh pot of saké that had just been brought.

"You'll have some, won't you?"

"Just a little."

Hidesaburô filled Okon's cup to the brim.

"You seem to be fond of a drink, Hidé," she commented

"Yes—since I married," he replied, downing his entire cup. Then, abruptly, Hidesaburô brought up the one subject Okon had hoped he wouldn't. "That *jôruri* singer, Shichinosuke—she didn't buy one of your hairpins, did she?"

Okon said nothing.

"Do you know why?" he asked.

Okon no longer felt in the mood to drink. She put her cup down on her tray just as Hidesaburô filled his one more time. "And you do, Hidé?"

"Uh-huh."

"Tell me—was it because it was too cheap?"

"She came knowing it was cheap."

"Then why?"

"Those silver chains are too long, Okon." Hidesaburô raised his cup to his mouth. Okon was too distracted to notice it needed filling. "You see," he continued, "when she performs *jôruri*, Shichinosuke shakes her head and the chains sway back and forth. But with chains as long as that, the audience will start looking at them and not at her."

Okon was silent.

"The same goes for that young lady walking by down there in the street—perhaps even more so. She wants a fancy hairpin to catch men's eyes but not one that stands out too much. Everyone knows that men are turned off by a woman who wears hairpins that are too fancy."

The scales fell from Okon's eyes. She realized she had been so intent on designing beautiful hairpins that she had forgotten the trick of how to make women beautiful. "And my pine tree design?" she blurted out. "Is that all right?"

Hidesaburô slowly placed his saké cup down on the tray in front of him and paused before answering. "Yes, that should sell nicely."

"Oh, good!" Okon closed her eyes and let out an audible sigh. How lucky she was to have an old friend she could rely on!

When she opened her eyes, however, Hidesaburô was staring at her. He must have been one of those rare individuals whose face didn't turn red when he drank alcohol, for in the light of the lantern his cheeks and forehead had a remarkably pallid glow, and his eyes were riveted on her.

With an awful premonition, Okon began to stand up but Hidesaburô's hand grabbed her sleeve and effortlessly pulled her toward him.

"What are you doing?" Okon struggled as she felt his lips running over the nape of her neck toward her cheek. They were unpleasantly cold and damp. "Stop it! We're just old friends, aren't we?"

"Can't old friends fall in love?"

For a brief moment, Okon stopped resisting. Just then Hidesaburô's lips found hers and, suddenly, they no longer felt cold to her.

But he has a wife and child.

"We can't!" Okon pushed Hidesaburô away with all her strength. With unexpected readiness, he released his grip. Okon retreated to the other side of the room, near the fusuma doors. After straightening her hair, she turned and looked at Hidesaburô. "Hidé, I . . . I thought our relationship was purely about business."

Without saying a word, Hidesaburô reached for his saké cup.

The red autumn leaves that had been splashed across the garden were now faded and shriveled, and had begun to fall. Already, the large brown leaves of the paulownia lay strewn across the stepping-stones leading from the house.

Okon had been crouching on the veranda for almost an hour. Omaki, bringing her some tea a little while earlier, must have assumed Okon was mulling over her hairpin design. She had quietly set the tray of tea and cakes down just outside the door to Okon's room and gone away.

Five days had passed since the incident with Hidesaburô. Not surprisingly, there had been no word from him since then. Okon returned to the sitting room with the tea tray. She picked up one of the cakes but changed her mind—she was in no mood to eat. She glanced at her desk, which was covered with sketches for her new design, and recalled that the silversmith had asked her to change the look of the snow on the pine needles.

Okon opened the box on her desk containing her inkstone and began rubbing a stick of ink against it. An image of Hidesaburô's face flashed before her eyes. Whether as children studying together in school or as adults running businesses of their own, Okon had never thought of Hidesaburô as anything other than a rival. And yet last night she had again dreamed of making love to him.

To get her mind off wanting to see Hidesaburô, Okon hastily began covering the paper in front of her with sketches. But it was no good. After working for a while, she would suddenly catch herself leaning over her desk with her head resting in her hands, daydreaming about kissing Hidesaburô or doodling pictures of his face.

Okon slapped herself on the cheeks with both hands and picked up her brush. I must finish the pine tree design right away, she told herself, but before she knew it she again found herself daydreaming with her chin in her hands.

Okon slapped herself on the cheeks once more. Just then, she heard animated voices coming from the back door. It was her hairdresser, Otoku. It sounded as though she was explaining to Omaki why she was late.

Okon smiled wryly to herself. She had completely forgotten that Otoku was coming to do her hair today. She could picture Otoku bowing obsequiously to Omaki as she began making her way through the house to Okon's room, bowing and scraping every step of the way, even going so far as to greet the errand boy as she passed him in the hallway.

"My, I *am* late, aren't I?" said Otoku, unraveling an apron wrapped around some fine-toothed combs as she entered the room. "At work already, then, are you, miss? I don't know where you get the energy! You're so dedicated to your work, and here I am always getting distracted by one thing or another. I really have no excuse—none at all . . ."

Otoku deluged Okon with her usual high-pitched, rapid-fire barrage of chatter. From now until the hairdresser was done combing and tying up her hair, Okon would have to sit and listen to the woman prattling on about all the neighborhood gossip: who had slipped and fallen on their backside in the street, which house had just given birth to a litter of kittens, and so on and so forth.

But as a hairdresser, Otoku was simply the best. The way she tied a topknot and made Okon's hair puff out in back was enough to make one swoon. And as for the woman's annoying chatter, today Okon would just have to grin and bear it, but by tomorrow even that would seem a welcome diversion as she poured over her account books and went about her other mundane tasks.

"I almost forgot, miss," Otoku lowered her voice just as she was about to leave. "The Tatsumiya's young master asked me to give you this."

Okon, who had been examining her coiffure in a small pocket mirror, watched as the woman placed what looked like a twisted up piece of paper in her lap. Then the hairdresser tapped herself on the chest and gave Okon a look that seemed to say, "Don't worry, miss, this is all between you and me."

Okon was about to blurt out that there must be some mistake, but Otoku raised a finger and gestured as though touching it to Okon's lips. Then she quickly rose and left the room. Okon heard her calling out Omaki's name. The maid apparently had asked the hairdresser to redo her own hair as well while she was there.

Okon undid the twist of paper, her fingers trembling slightly. On the back of what looked like a voided sales slip was written, "Tonight, six o'clock at The Palace on the pond in Ueno." The Palace was one of a number of teahouses on the island in the middle of Shinobazu Pond that was used for lovers' trysts.

Does he seriously think that I'll go?

Okon took her brush and blotted out all but the first three words, then tossed the note into the wastepaper basket. It infuriated her that Hidesaburô would expect her to come just like that without even bothering to ask if it was convenient for her or requesting a reply. She picked up the stick of ink that was resting against her inkstone and mechanically began rubbing it against the stone. Then she remembered that she had finished preparing her ink before Otoku arrived.

No sooner had she picked up her brush than the next thing she knew she was again leaning on her desk with her chin propped against her left arm. Okon took out a fresh sheet of paper and started sketching pine needles over and over without any snow. She was still struggling with it when the bell outside sounded four o'clock.

Since the bell tolled six times between sunrise and sunset throughout the year, the hours as measured were shorter in winter due to the decline in daylight. By the time Okon finished redoing her makeup and changing into a nice kimono to go out in, it would probably already be five o'clock. She raced over to her dresser, hurriedly opened one of the drawers, and took out a kimono with a fishing-weir print design. Then, one by one, she held up the end of each of her sashes against the kimono, trying to find one that matched. Though they had all been made especially to go with her various outfits, none seemed to be the right color. Beads of sweat began to stand out on her forehead.

Finally, she settled on a reddish brown sash that she often wore, and dashed out to the kitchen to get some hot water. After washing her face, she painstakingly applied her makeup.

Okon left the shop, telling the head clerk on her way out that something had suddenly come up. She hailed a palanquin and took it across Nihonbashi Bridge into Muromachi, where she got out and sent it on its way.

At the teahouse, Hidesaburô was waiting for her in a dimly lit

room. He was seated at an open window staring out at the darkened
pond, just as before.

―୧ჯ୨―

As a matter of fact, it was not the first time Okon had been to one of
Shinobazu Pond's infamous teahouses. Before her father had broken
off her engagement, she had crossed the threshold of one such establishment at the invitation of her fiancé. That had been when she was
sixteen. Since then she had not even been to pray at the island's Benten
Shrine, let alone set foot in one of its teahouses.

She alighted from her palanquin a short distance from the pond
and passed on foot through the torii gate at the entrance to the cause-
way leading out to the island. Ahead, she saw the lantern on which was
written the name of the teahouse. As she approached, however, her
steps had faltered. After checking to see that no one was about, and
sweating profusely from sheer embarrassment, she darted through the
split curtain hanging in the entranceway. As it turned out, Hidesaburô
had been watching her calmly from the window the whole time.

He's using me—I know that.

"Come," Hidesaburô had said, reaching out his hand to her. She
had clung desperately to him, all the while thinking that when it was
over she would not simply be able to go back to her work as though
nothing had happened. He gave her a look that seemed to say, "Is it
your first time?" She shook her head. Then she took Hidesaburô's hand
and guided it into the opening of her kimono. Hidesaburô told her to
undo her sash, and they made love.

As expected, she was in no mood for work the next day. And, as
she had feared, she waited and waited but Otoku failed to appear with
a message from Hidesaburô. She gave up trying to think about her
design and instead went and poked her head into the shop. Perhaps
it was just her imagination, but the Sasaya's head clerk and the other
employees seemed cold and distant toward her. They must have been
sick and tired of hearing her go on and on about her new hairpin for
The Okon Collection, with as yet nothing to show for it.

Unable to bear it any longer, Okon went out into the street. A
fierce winter wind whipped dust and sand past her, causing the Sasaya's

signboard to sway back and forth. If her pine tree design wasn't finished soon, it would soon be the wrong season to try to sell it. Okon closed her eyes and tried to think, but the only thing that popped into her head was the memory of what had transpired at the teahouse.

If I don't finish this hairpin . . .

In fact, it would probably make little difference to the Sasaya's business. Things would revert to the way they had always been back when the Sasaya sold only high-priced merchandise, and the head clerk would take over the running of the shop.

Okon would go from being a woman who hadn't gotten married to a woman who couldn't get married. She would go from sitting at her desk day in and day out designing hairpins to whiling away her time in the middle of her big room, occasionally drinking a cup of tea brought by Omaki and listening to the creaking of the timbers and the rustling of the leaves in the garden.

"What nonsense!" The wind carried off Okon's voice. She felt an urge to laugh. The Sasaya's errand boy came out of the shop and looked in Okon's direction with a strange expression. Following his eyes, Okon turned her head and saw a man with a determined look on his face standing a short distance off. It was Hei'emon the cotton merchant—her old friend Heita.

"Why, hello," Okon said. She batted her eyelids several times so as not to let on she was in a bad mood. "Why didn't you say something earlier instead of just standing there?"

"I did—several times." Heita looked surprised. "Well, never mind that. I just happened to be in the neighborhood, and since I haven't had a chance to eat lunch yet I wondered if you might like to join me?"

"It's fine with me, but I don't have anything very good to offer you."

"I'm not asking you to make lunch for me—I wanted to get some broiled eel over there." Heita smiled wryly and pointed up the street toward the second block of Okechô. There was a new eel restaurant that had opened recently just off the main street. Heita waited as Okon told the errand boy where she was going, then he began slowly walking down the street.

As soon as they turned off the main street Okon spotted the eel restaurant's signboard. It was already past three o'clock—too late for lunch but too early for dinner—and there were no other customers in the restaurant's second-floor dining room. It suddenly occurred to her that Heita perhaps knew about her and Hidesaburô. She peered at his face while pretending to look around the room, but Heita was ordering some saké from the waitress and didn't notice her gaze directed at him.

The waitress went back downstairs, leaving the two of them alone. Heita sat cross-legged with his hands resting on his knees, his thumbs tracing circles on the fabric of his clothing. It appeared to be a habit of his.

"So what did you want to talk about?" asked Okon, trying to control her voice, but the words came out sounding strained nonetheless.

"Er, well . . ." Heita's thumbs continued to trace circles on his knees.

"Is it about Hidesaburô?"

"Yes." Heita's voice was surprisingly calm. "He's done something really despicable."

"What do you mean?"

"He was jealous of you, Okon." Okon couldn't imagine what Hidesaburô would have to be jealous about. She remained silent and waited for Heita to continue. "You see, you and your family own the Sasaya—even if one or two of your hairpins isn't a success, you can always try again. But Hidé's just the son-in-law of the Tatsumiya's owner. His father-in-law won't let him run the business the way he wants to, even though those personalized candles of his were a huge success."

"And he's jealous of me because of that?"

"That's what he said."

"But then . . ." Without realizing it, Okon raised her voice. "But then why did he sleep with me? I told him I wanted our relationship to be strictly about business."

"Because—"

Just then the waitress appeared with Heita's saké and a small dish of pickled vegetables. He immediately picked up a cup and began filling it. Then he waited for the sound of the waitress's retreating footsteps to fade away before he resumed speaking.

"Because he knew that being young and innocent it would interfere with your work—here, have a drink," Heita said, placing the cup in Okon's hand. Then, in the same emotionless tone, he asked, "Are you in love with him?" Heita refilled Okon's cup before pouring some saké into his own. "Because if you are really in love with Hidé I could seduce his wife."

"Huh?"

"What I mean is, I could break up his marriage," Heita said, smiling, a mischievous look on his face. "After all, I'm not exactly unattractive to the ladies, if you know what I mean."

"I can see that. But isn't it a capital offense to sleep with another man's wife?"

"Well, only if the authorities get wind of it." Heita emptied his saké cup in one gulp. "And Hidé would never let that happen. But if he knew I had slept with his wife, he wouldn't be able to stand it. It would destroy his relationship with Ochie, and drive him from her house."

"What terrible things you think of."

With his eyes still lowered, Heita refilled Okon's saké cup. "Well, you know, Okon . . ." Heita paused to refill his own cup. At last, he looked up at her face. "Even if I say so myself, my life is nothing to complain about. I have a good wife, adorable kids. That's why I don't want to see you get hurt. As for me, I've never thought of you as a rival—not even once."

Okon put her cup to her lips. She swallowed it all in one gulp, feeling the saké flowing down her throat and into her stomach.

"Shall I order us another round?" As Heita held the flask of warm saké over Okon's cup, the smell of grilled eel wafted up from the kitchen below.

—⚬⚬—

Okon walked with Heita as far as the foot of Nihonbashi Bridge. They had drunk a second flask of saké, then another, and another. In the end they had polished off seven and half flasks in all. Okon had not even noticed that they kept repeating the same conversation over and over. Even Heita, who hadn't seemed the least bit drunk in the restaurant, looked precariously unsteady on his feet once they had left.

"All right then, I'll drop in on you again sometime. Remember, I'll seduce the Tatsumiya's mistress for you anytime you want!"

"Not so loud—people will hear you!"

"I don't care who hears me!"

"Just hurry up and get home. Oito must be wondering where you are."

"I know, I know."

Okon watched as Heita disappeared into the evening crush of pedestrians, a small wooden box of grilled eel dangling from one hand, then she dashed back to the Sasaya. Entering the house through the side door, she raced down the corridor past the back garden and into her room. Then she put her face down on her desk and began to cry, the tears she had been trying so hard to hold back streaming down her cheeks as though a dam had burst.

Okon sobbed loudly. But whether it was joy over Heita's feelings for her, longing for Hidesaburô, or bitterness at being duped by him, she didn't know. She just knew she wanted to weep for all she was worth.

After crying for some time, she lifted her head from her desk and looked up. The pine tree design that had eluded her seemed to appear before her eyes. *Well, if they think they can make fun of me because I'm a woman, they're making a big mistake.* She would see to it the hairpin was a success and made lots of money for the Sasaya. Hidesaburô could stamp the ground in frustration all he wanted—he'd never be able to compete with her.

On the other hand, thought Okon, maybe he'll come and buy one.

V

︎︎ FORGET-ME-NOT ︎︎

The cries emanating from the sideshow stalls sounded somehow more subdued than usual. The stalls were probably less crowded today on account of the leaden sky, which seemed to threaten snow.

Oichi was seated leaning against a charcoal brazier listening distractedly to the distant hubbub when she heard the sounds of footsteps coming up the stairs. She was on the second floor of the Kagaya, a book wholesaler's in Yonezawachô, on the south side of Hirokôji in Ryôgoku.

Oichi sat up straight. There were two sets of footsteps, one clearly belonging to the proprietor of the Kagaya, Kichiemon, whose short legs labored under the weight of his large body, and the other to his head clerk, Rihachi.

Kichiemon was known for two things: being extremely fat, and turning Utagawa Kuniyoshi, the master painter and printmaker to whom Oichi had been apprenticed, into a bestselling ukiyo-e artist. Before Kichiemon got hold of him, Kuniyoshi's book illustrations and portraits of actors and beautiful women had fallen out of favor and no publisher would come near him. Then Kichiemon had asked him to create a series of warrior prints called *The One Hundred and Eight Heroes of The Water Margin*. The series had been an unprecedented success, propelling Kuniyoshi into the top ranks of Edo ukiyo-e artists and bringing fame to the Kagaya.

Yesterday Kichiemon had dispatched a messenger to Oichi's house to say he wanted to speak to her about publishing a new series of colored woodblock prints the following year. Thinking Kichiemon must have something interesting in mind, Oichi set off from home at noon to ensure she wouldn't be late for the appointment.

"Sorry to keep you waiting." The shoji leading into the room slid open.

Poorly lit even at the best of times, the corridor outside the room was that much darker due to the gloomy sky leaden with clouds. Kichiemon entered the room and kneeled just inside the door, his lips slightly parted in a smile between his flabby cheeks. Behind him Rihachi, thin and wan in contrast, flashed Oichi a broad and affable grin. They exchanged the conventional greetings, lamenting the recent bad weather. Then Kichiemon, who always wore the same expression regardless of his mood, furrowed his brow.

"It's really very sad about Yohei, isn't it?" he said.

Oichi nodded silently. Yohei, her father, had passed away at the end of September. Now the year was drawing to a close and she would soon be marking the one-hundredth day since his death.

"How old was he?"

"Forty-five—no, -six. Oh, how awful of me, forgetting my own father's age! You must think me a terrible daughter!" laughed Oichi, covering her mouth with the back of her hand. She was rather taken aback at her voice echoing through the room.

"He was very much in his prime, wasn't he?" commented Rihachi. "You must be sad to be all on your own now."

"I'd be lying if I said I wasn't. But now I don't have to look after him any more, I've got more time for my work. Oh my! If Father's ghost hears that he'll say, 'What do you mean? I was the one looking after *you!*' and give me a good slap!" she added, hunching her shoulders as though expecting the blow at any moment. This time it was Rihachi who burst out laughing.

Kichiemon waited for the clerk to regain his composure, then turned and looked at him. Nodding, Rihachi crawled forward on his knees and spread a piece of paper out on the tatami before Oichi. On it was a list of place names in the city of Edo. Oichi gave Kichiemon an expectant look, urging him to continue.

"Miss Yoshihana, I'd like you to draw a series of one hundred famous views of Edo."

Kichiemon leaned his fat body forward with obvious discomfort and peered at the list of names. "Yoshihana"—short for Utagawa Yoshihana—was the name Oichi's teacher, Utagawa Kuniyoshi, had given her.

That year, 1833, Hoeidô, a small book wholesaler in Shiochô on Reiganjima, a small island in the mouth of the Sumida River, had teamed up with the venerable publishing house Tsuruya Senkakudô to publish a series of landscape prints by Hiroshige under the title *The Fifty-Three Stations of the Tôkaidô*. The success of the series had rivaled that of Kuniyoshi's *Heroes of The Water Margin*. Now other book dealers, hoping to repeat Hiroshige's success, were clamoring to commission Edo's best artists to create similar series featuring the Tôkaidô, the Nakasendô, and other major highways. There was even a rumor that Hoeidô was thinking of moving from Reiganjima to a more central location in the heart of Edo proper.

Kichiemon, however, maintained that he wanted nothing to do with "highway" pictures for the time being. Edo would become very dull indeed, he asserted, if in front of every bookshop in the city there were nothing but a monotonous succession of highway scenes.

"What do you think?" Kichiemon looked at Oichi. He seemed less concerned as to whether she would accept the commission than whether or not she was satisfied with the list of places they had drawn up.

Oichi gave a vague nod.

The fact was that the previous year Kuniyoshi and Hiroshige, prior to the latter's publication of *The Fifty-Three Stations of the Tôkaidô*, had each issued his own series of prints entitled *Famous Views of the Eastern Capital*. Kuniyoshi's version had enjoyed considerable popularity among other ukiyo-e artists, and even Oichi herself had admired it enough to go out and purchase a set. But its sales had not lived up to expectations. Oichi had heard that even Hiroshige's version had not sold much until the success of his *Tôkaidô* series.

The timing was bad, Oichi thought to herself. Over the past year there had been reports of crop failures in Japan's northeastern provinces. When rice became expensive, people stopped buying woodblock prints of familiar scenes unless it was something that really grabbed their attention. Hiroshige's *Tôkaidô* prints had offered Edo's inhabitants gorgeous depictions of strange and distant places. It had been a big hit because it allowed people to forget, if only for a brief moment, the lamentable state of their rice chests and their pocket books.

Rice was now even more expensive than the year before. If Kuniyoshi had been forced to abandon his series after the Kagaya had issued just ten prints, how did Oichi suppose her series of one hundred views of Edo could succeed?

"I know prints by women artists don't sell well even at the best of times," said Kichiemon, never one to mince words, "but you're an exception, Miss Yoshihana." From Kichiemon's expression, it was hard for Oichi to tell what he was really thinking. However, his words didn't strike her as mere flattery. "In any case," he continued, "we can't expect a huge success like *Heroes of The Water Margin,* but I'm willing to bet it will do quite well. I must say, I think the treatment of landscape in your prints of beautiful women is very fine indeed."

"It's kind of you to say so."

"Plus, these days people are buying books with pictures of geishas, not samurai. That's why *The Plum Calendar* has become more popular than *The Water Margin.* So with your knack for drawing women, Miss Yoshihana, I think you're a better bet right now than Master Kuniyoshi and his warriors."

Oichi ran her eyes over the places on the list: the Sumida River, Asakusa, Ochanomizu . . . From the hasty scrawl, it appeared that Rihachi had jotted them down as quickly as they had popped into his head. Oichi pictured in her mind the prints Kuniyoshi and Hiroshige had made of these places. Kuniyoshi's landscapes had a unique, human sensibility all their own, while Hiroshige's were suffused with tranquility and calm.

Oichi knew she would never measure up to these great masters— she mustn't let herself get carried away by Kichiemon's flattering remarks. At the same time, she sensed her own view of landscape was unique from anything Kuniyoshi or Hiroshige had ever dreamed of. She started to feel an urge to try her hand at a series of her own.

"What we want," Kichiemon said, "are pictures that will open people's eyes—make them realize what a wonderful place Edo is to live. The places on this list are just suggestions. If you don't care for them, Miss Yoshihana, please feel free to come up with your own."

"I understand. I think I would prefer to choose them myself."

Kichiemon again turned and gave Rihachi a look, this time one that seemed to say, "If she produces any pictures you like, send them over to the block carver straight away."

Oichi unconsciously let out a deep sigh. She realized her heart was racing. Of course, she knew it was beating with joy at having received so large a commission. But deep down something was nagging at her.

Rihachi opened the shoji and called downstairs. From the reply, it seemed the meal was ready.

"You don't mind if we join you, do you?" joked Kichiemon, a smile playing about the corners of his mouth. "Now, if Yohei were alive he'd probably have given me another good scolding just now."

Oichi cocked her head coyly to one side.

"I can almost hear Yohei muttering, 'There she goes again,'" Rihachi chimed in from over Kichiemon's shoulder. "'She'll never find herself a husband now!'"

"He'd never have said a thing like that," Oichi responded, shaking her head and waving her hand in denial. "After all, it was my father who went to the Kagaya and convinced you to ask Master Kuniyoshi to make me his apprentice. And he only did that because he'd already given up on the idea of marrying me off. 'Harder than putting roof tiles on an upside-down house,' he used to say!"

"That's not the impression I got," retorted Rihachi, laughing. "Four or five days before he passed away, he stopped by our shop on his way home from work. He said with a rueful smile that he wished he'd found you a good man you could rely on—not someone to teach you how to draw woodblock prints."

"My, was he that disappointed?" said Oichi with another peal of laughter. "And to think how I used to say I'd rather make one good print than live in misery with a boring husband—and Father would nod in agreement and reply, 'Indeed, indeed'!"

"Your father was one of the best roof-tilers in the business," noted Kichiemon. "With him gone there's no one I'd want to tile our roof when we rebuild our shop."

Oichi looked away. Just yesterday, Kuniyoshi had said the very same thing to her.

There was a lull in the conversation during which the listless shouts from the sideshow stalls drifted into the room. Rihachi slipped out and went downstairs, presumably to find out why their lunch hadn't arrived.

—☙☙—

As Oichi returned to her house in Yokoamichô in Edo's Honjô district, the nearby bell was just sounding four in the afternoon.

Darkness hung over the corners of the room, and Oichi decided she ought to light a lamp. But first, without even bothering to change out of her kimono, she went and crouched beside the charcoal brazier. The room felt very cold without a fire burning or the warmth of another human body in the house.

Oichi drew the charcoal bucket toward her and began poking about in the ashes of the brazier for the smoldering ember she had buried there earlier. Crossing Ryôgoku Bridge, a chill wind had whipped across her path and frozen her to the bone. Now the fire tongs she held in her hands refused to do her bidding. Pausing several times to breathe onto her hands, she transferred some charcoal from the bucket to the brazier. On top of it she placed the ember she had at last found among the ashes. Pursing her lips, she blew on the ember until the edges of the charcoal began to glow. Then she placed an iron kettle over the fire. Her neck and shoulders felt stiff and tense, and she began moving her head about in circles, trying to relax.

What an exhausting meeting that was!

After lunch, instead of the customary sake, light green tea had been served along with some sweets from the Fujimura. Oichi had talked and laughed a lot, so much so that Rihachi had teased her saying that the tea must have made her drunk. Carried away by the sound of her own voice, she had completely forgotten to look for an opportunity to take her leave. No doubt Kichiemon and Rihachi had been struggling to find an excuse to bring things to a close and make their exit.

Since her father's death, Oichi found that she got carried away whenever she was in the company of others. She knew that the excitement would tire her out, and when she was tired out she dreaded having to go home to her lonely, empty house—but still she let herself get carried away. At home, there was no one to talk to. Even if she announced that she had just received a commission for a series of one hundred woodblock prints, her words would only be swallowed up in the darkness of the small, four-and-a-half mat room. When she was with others, Oichi didn't want to have to go home, and in the back of her mind she thought that if she acted like the life of the party her companions wouldn't want her to go home either.

"If only Father were still here . . ."

Yohei had been a man of few words, a trait that had earned him the nickname "the Clam." Even if he were alive and Oichi were to tell him about her new commission, he wouldn't have said "congratulations" or anything like that. Instead, as he sat eating his dinner, his sunburned face would have broken into a smile and he would simply have held out a cup of saké for her. She wished she could see Yohei's smiling face again. Then she wouldn't have to act like the life of the party whenever she was out with others. And she would be able to forget about Saijirô, whom she hadn't heard from for some time now.

In fact, she hadn't even spoken with Saijirô since about a month before her father had died. He had put in an appearance at Yohei's wake but had hurried off right after lighting some incense in front of the altar, mumbling something about how busy he was now that he had gone into business as a woodblock carver on his own.

Now, some three months later, she had heard a rumor at the Kagaya that Saijirô already had four apprentices of his own. The test of a block cutter's skill was how well he could do women's hairlines, and Saijirô was so good at such details that people called him "Silky Strand Saiji." From what Oichi had heard, there were plenty of ukiyo-e artists who specifically asked for Saijirô by name, and students were banging on his door begging to become his apprentices.

But compared to before, when he himself had been apprenticed to Yasugorô, it should have become easier for Saijirô to find time to meet Oichi. Recently, Rihachi had told her that he had run into Saijirô apparently on his way to the archery range to unwind a little. So it seemed Saijirô had time to shoot arrows but not to see her! Or perhaps . . . Oichi began to suspect there was another reason. Saijirô was now a married man with a wife and child—maybe he had come to regard Oichi as a burden now that her father was dead and she was all on her own.

Movement finally started to return to Oichi's numb fingers. She stretched out on the tatami and reached for the oil lamp. The floor felt cold through her kimono, but it was too much trouble to stand up. The lamp was empty, however, and the container of oil was in the kitchen. Now that her body had finally warmed up a little, she was loath to go into the frigid kitchen. Since she was alone, there wasn't really any need to bother lighting the lamp as long as she didn't mind sitting in the dark. Oichi curled up her body into a ball and held her hands out in front of the brazier.

From the street came the sound of wooden clogs running past the house. "It's outrageous!" she heard a voice say. "These days a hundred *mon* only buys seven and a half *gô* of rice."

At one time, a hundred *mon* would have bought twelve or thirteen *gô*. Then it fell to ten and later nine. Now the price of rice had nearly doubled and a hundred *mon* only bought seven and a half *gô*. Widespread starvation was inevitable. Just the other day, Oichi had heard a rumor that riots and looting had broken out in Shinagawa. What would become of her if her *One Hundred Views of Edo* turned out to be a flop? A cold shiver ran down her spine. As Kichiemon had said, Oichi had indeed made a name for herself as an ukiyo-e artist, but she had never had a big success like *Heroes of The Water Margin*. If her new series didn't sell, she would soon find that publishers would have nothing to do with her.

"Well, better get to work!" Oichi slapped her cheeks to shake off her listlessness and stood up.

Suddenly she heard the lattice front door being slid open. Then a voice called out asking if anyone was home. *It can't be,* Oichi thought. It sounded like Saijirô's voice. She could count on the fingers of one hand the number of times Saijirô had visited her house. He had only ever dropped by when he needed to change the time or place of their next meeting. Even then he would only stand in the doorway and quickly make his excuses before rushing off.

Again the voice called out inquiring if anyone was home. This time there could be no mistake. Flustered, Oichi was about to reply but stopped herself. Wasn't this the same man who for three months since her father's death hadn't once shown his face? She wasn't about to welcome him with open arms. Just then she heard him say, "Careless of her to leave the place unlocked." Seeing there were no lamps lit, he must have assumed she was out. If she said nothing Saijirô would leave. Oichi quickly smoothed down a few wayward strands of hair before opening the shoji.

Saijirô was on his way out, but now turned back. His cheeks looked a bit hollow, probably from overwork. Oichi had intended to cheerfully call out to him, "Fancy seeing you again!" Instead, she kneeled on the wooden floor just outside the room and said nothing.

"Please excuse my long silence," Saijirô said, sounding very formal. "Actually, I've been wondering how you've been getting along since your father's death."

"I see . . ." Oichi replied, her voice breaking. She wanted to say straightforwardly, "I've been fine" or "Don't worry about me," but the words wouldn't come out.

Saijirô looked away uneasily. "I meant to come by sooner, but something always seems to come up. It doesn't look as though I'll be able to attend the ceremony for the one-hundredth-day anniversary of your father's death, so I've come to offer some incense. I apologize for dropping by unannounced like this."

"I see . . ."

"I'll come inside," Saijirô said, seeming to lose patience with Oichi's reticence. He stepped over the threshold. "Is it all right if I come in?"

"Please do," replied Oichi.

The lamp was still unlit and the room was as dark as a cave.

Awkwardly mumbling something about having dozed off, Oichi lit the lamp. When she turned around, Saijirô was kneeling at the Buddhist altar with his hands together in prayer, having placed the offering he had brought in front of it. Oichi expected him to say he would have to leave right away, but she went ahead and placed the kettle over the brazier to make tea, having poured half of the water out so it would boil quickly.

The smell of incense wafted through the room. Saijirô again put his hands together in prayer before moving away from the altar. Giving no clear sign whether he was leaving or staying, he rose to his knees and began rubbing his hands together, as though they were still numb. Oichi turned her face toward him and their eyes met. Saijirô seemed to have been waiting to catch her eye so he could speak.

"I'm relieved to see you're in good spirits."

"Me, in good spirits?" she said. Her voice sounded reproachful. "How could I be, considering I've been waiting for you all this time?"

"But I've been busy."

"I see."

Once again they both fell quiet. It had become strangely silent outside in the street, as though it was about to start snowing. Oichi tried to think of something to say. Then she noticed Saijirô had sat down again with his knees together and was struggling to broach something on his mind.

"Um, listen . . ." He seemed unsure whether to address her as "Oichi" or "Yoshihana." After a brief pause he began again. "I'm sure you must think it's a bit late for me to be saying this, but if there's anything I can do for you just let me know."

Oichi looked at Saijirô. He seemed deliberately to have turned his face away from her and the lamp cast a shadow upon it.

"I'm not sure exactly how I should put this," he continued, "but . . . well, I feel like I owe you an apology." Perhaps coming to pay his respects to her father was just a pretext. Perhaps this was the real reason he had come. "For what it's worth, I'll do whatever I can to help."

"Thank you."

Oichi began thinking of the places she wanted to include in her *One Hundred Views of Edo*. What a help it would be if Saijirô would agree to carve the blocks! What confidence it would give her if he were beside her, advising her on what scenes to choose! She had intended to remain silent on the subject, but she went ahead and told Saijirô about the commission she had just received.

"A series of one hundred prints, you say?"

"That's right."

"Good for you!" Saijirô said, sidling up to the brazier. "But it won't be easy, you know. Kuniyoshi's prints didn't sell because they were too commonplace. And Hiroshige's . . . well, personally I didn't dislike them, but some people said they were too 'pretty.'"

"But I'm not them, I'm me."

"You'd better go out and make some sketches."

"I intend to—even if the washing and cleaning gets neglected for a while."

"But be careful. There've been rumors about riots."

"Will you come with me?"

"Sure, why not? Just give me four or five days—I'm in the middle of an urgent job."

The kettle started to boil. Oichi put the tea leaves into an earthenware pot and clumsily poured in the water from the kettle. When it was done steeping, the tea looked bitter. Saijirô, however, drank it down with gusto before announcing that it was time for him to go. Once he had said he was leaving, Saijirô was not the type of man to brook any further discussion. Oichi saw him off at the front door and, worrying about tomorrow's weather, stood waiting until he was out of sight. Then she returned to the four-and-a-half-mat room.

The warmth of another human body still lingered in the room— the warmth of Saijirô's body.

—⌘—

When Oichi's father Yohei had been alive, they had often eaten simmered tofu. Busy working away on a picture, she would postpone the dinner preparations until very late.

"That's okay. Let's just have tofu." Returning from his workshop,

Yohei never betrayed any signs of annoyance. It had been that way ever since Oichi had done *The Seven Beauties of the Bamboo Grove*.

The Seven Beauties had been her breakthrough work, a triptych of seven beautiful women. She could still remember the expression on Yohei's face when it had been published.

"My, you've got real talent, haven't you!" he had exclaimed, his usually severe expression replaced by one of obvious delight. That was probably the only time she had seen her father completely enraptured.

The Seven Beauties had been carved by Saijirô. Oichi had met him for the first time the previous spring, when she was sixteen. She had gone to Bakurochô in Nihonbashi with her finished pictures ready to be made into prints. She was to deliver them to the Yamaguchiya Kinkôdô, a shop specializing in Edo books, and it was there she had met Saijirô who had come to collect the drawings. That had been four years ago.

Saijirô had taken Oichi's drawings, shoved them into the breast of his kimono with an irritated look on his face, and left the room. From observing her father and her father's friends, Oichi knew artisans were an unsociable lot. But Saijirô's manner went beyond unsociable—it was downright arrogant. Feeling as though she had been told that he didn't have time to waste hanging about with some young girl like her, Oichi shot out of the room after him. If Tôhei, the Yamaguchiya's proprietor, hadn't called her back, she would certainly have chased after Saijirô and demanded her pictures back.

She had thus been left with the impression that Saijirô was a most disagreeable man. Then, not long afterward, she met him again. Her teacher, Kuniyoshi, had invited her over to his house, located in a part of Shin Izumichô that everyone referred to as Gen'yadana. On the way there she ran into Saijirô.

The sky had looked like rain, but just as she was leaving the house she had seen some gaps peeking through the clouds and had decided at the last minute to leave her umbrella behind. That had been a mistake. Just as she reached Takasagochô it began to rain. Oichi ducked under some eaves for a moment to get out of the rain. But as it was not coming down all that hard and she didn't want to be late for her appointment, she draped a handkerchief over her head and dashed off again through the rain.

Saijirô had caught up with her, calling out her name. He had an umbrella with him that he held tucked under his arm instead of over his head. Oichi muttered something in reply and looked away. He was the last person whose company she wanted.

"Here."

He held out his umbrella to her. Blinking, Oichi looked at him. He wore an easy smile, quite unlike the man she had met at the Yamaguchiya.

"Please, take it."

He opened the umbrella and put it into her hand. There were raindrops on it — he must have spotted her hurrying along in the rain and closed his umbrella so he could chase after her.

Oichi said nothing. Unfazed by her silence Saijirô continued, "You paint very well, Miss Yoshihana."

Oichi blinked again.

"I'm afraid I was terribly rude the other day at the Yamaguchiya," Saijirô said, shaking his head to refuse the umbrella that Oichi was trying to return to him. "It shames me to say this, but I spent ten years patiently biding my time before I was allowed to carve heads and faces. But no sooner did I feel I'd become a full-fledged craftsman than I began to find fault with other people's work."

Oichi still did not speak.

"Lately," he continued, "even famous artists have completely lost the ability to depict women with any sensuality—the hands and feet are all wrong. I can't help but get angry when I have to carve some second-rate picture. But then . . ." he paused. "I was astonished when I saw your pictures, Miss Yoshihana. I won't say they were perfect, but at least you'd managed to get the hands and feet just right. It's been a long time since I carved a print with as much enthusiasm as I did yours."

Oichi heard the sound of rain striking the umbrella.

"It's really started coming down now. A moment ago when I saw you out here, I thought we can't have a fine artist like her getting soaked and catching a cold, now can we!"

Oichi's negative impression of Saijirô had completely vanished. She held the umbrella over him. One of Kuniyoshi's older apprentices—also apparently on his way to the master's house—passed them in the street and said something teasingly to Oichi.

"You're just jealous!" she shot back at him. Saijirô looked embarrassed.

It didn't take long for the two to become lovers. The only thing that prevented rumors from getting about was that everyone thought of Oichi as being indifferent to romance—the type of girl who wasn't embarrassed to be seen sharing an umbrella with a man. Saijirô told her there was someone else he had been seeing but that he had ended the relationship. Oichi interpreted his remark to mean that he was interested in marrying her. In fact, that had been his original intention. The two had even gone looking for a house to rent together near Yasugorô's workshop in Aioichô where Saijirô worked.

And yet Saijirô had gone and married the other woman—Onobu was her name—even after saying they had broken up. Apparently she had been carrying Saijirô's child. Oichi resigned herself to her fate. For whatever reason, Saijirô had forsaken her. There was no point losing sleep over a man who had thrown her aside. All she wanted was to be able to inform him, gracefully, that their relationship was over. But for some reason she could not bring herself to do it.

Once she had even stood waiting on a corner in Aioichô until sunset, hoping she might run into him. Another time, when she had heard that her publisher had commissioned Yasugorô to carve one of her pictures, she had intentionally inserted a mistake in it and used this as a pretext to go round to his workshop to see Saijirô. On that occasion Saijirô had not had the strength to cast Oichi aside. Instead, he had agreed to meet her later at the neighborhood Inari Shrine to talk. But once there, Oichi had broken down in tears, so Saijirô had led her to a nearby sweet shop. After eating a bowl of sweet *oshiruko* they had decided to move to a restaurant with a private room. When all was said and done, they had not been able to end the relationship. From then on, Oichi was always complaining she didn't see Saijirô enough, while he was always trying to put her off saying, "Don't you have any work you should be doing rather than seeing me?"

"I'm not being a home-wrecker, am I, Father?" Oichi had asked Yohei.

At dinner, after her father had learned from Oichi that the man she was in love with was a woodblock carver with a wife and child, he had sat drinking his saké without saying a word for the rest of the evening. The next day, too, he ate his breakfast in silence before heading off to work. He returned in the evening, clearly in a bad mood. Without even a word of greeting, he took the towel and wash bucket from Oichi and headed off to the bathhouse.

She thought perhaps he intended never to speak to her again, but when he returned he said down next to the brazier and said simply, "This guy of yours, does he do good work? Because if he's the type of guy whose work is suffering because he's torn between you and his wife, then she's welcome to him. He doesn't deserve you."

"In that case, you must mean it's okay for me to love Saijirô," Oichi said, drawing herself up and taking a sip of Yohei's saké.

Saijirô had earned his nickname "Silky Strand Saiji" once he had begun carving heads and faces. Kuniyoshi and the equally famous Kunisada—both of whom had been apprentices of the great Utagawa Toyokuni—had started asking for Saijirô by name. It was even rumored that the relationship between Saijirô and his boss, Yasugorô, had soured as a result.

One day, when Oichi went to the teahouse for her usual assignation with Saijirô, the first words out of his mouth had been, "You've outdone yourself this time, Oichi!" He was referring to her *Seven Beauties*. "I'll make this my best work ever!" Saijirô had repeated over and over as he made love to her.

True to his word, Saijirô had done a magnificent job. *The Seven Beauties* was a popular theme at the time parodying the classic theme *The Seven Sages of the Bamboo Grove* by replacing the usual Chinese sages with famous Edo beauties. Oichi's version had featured the Takemoto *jôruri* singers Kosen and Shichinosuke, the calligrapher Hasegawa Rikô, and Okon, proprietress of the Sasaya, a famous Nihonbashi boutique. The success of Oichi's *Seven Beauties* was attributable mainly to its freshness and her novel choices of women, yet it was undeniable that Saijirô's workmanship had played an important role as well. The way he had carved Okon of the Sasaya, for example, one could practically smell the scented perfume wafting from her hair as she stuck an ornamental hairpin into it.

Her teacher Kuniyoshi had complimented the work in his own idiosyncratic way, saying, "If only I could draw like that! Perhaps *you* should be teaching *me!*" Yamaguchiya Tôhei, Oichi's publisher, had also praised it and even her *gesaku*-writer friends had called it "a very fine piece of work." In those days she had been able to see Saijirô once every five—no, once every three days, and she felt that as long as they worked as a team there was no limit to what she could accomplish.

But over time she heard less and less frequently from Saijirô. When they did meet, he would announce as soon as they had finished making love that he had to go, leaving Oichi behind at the teahouse. No doubt Onobu was at home waiting up for him. I've become nothing but a fling to him, she thought. How many times had she cried bitterly to herself? How many times had she chucked the brushes and inks he had given her into the wastebasket, resolving to end their relationship? But her resolution was always short-lived, and when he sent for her she would go to him, fooling herself into thinking, "This time I'll really end it once and for all."

The pot of tofu on the brazier had come to a boil. Oichi scooped some onto a dish and turned to look at the Buddhist altar. She knew she couldn't rely on Saijirô, but as soon as she saw his face she would want to throw herself at him. No doubt Yohei was looking down at her with a rueful smile on his face.

―◦◦◦―

The observance of the one-hundredth-day anniversary of Yohei's death was held with Utagawa Kuniyoshi and Kagaya Kichiemon both in attendance. But there had been no word at all from Saijirô who, when they last met, had promised to get in touch with her again in four or five days. He had not even sent a message explaining that he was busy. Oichi put down her brush. Saijirô couldn't have forgotten his promise to her. After all, he had already been given her scenes of Oumayagashi and Hikagechô to carve.

Oichi's pictures had apparently exceeded Kichiemon's wildest expectations. The one of Oumayagashi showed two boys waiting for the ferryboat—one crouching at the water's edge and the other, grown restless, chasing cicadas—with the boat off in the distance. Her scene of Hikagechô captured a woman at the edge of the frame poking her head out from a side street lined with used-clothing shops during a break in her housework. Oichi had heard that Kichiemon delivered the drawings to Saijirô's workshop in person. She had been sure that when Saijirô saw Kichiemon's excitement he would come and take her out sketching, even if only so that he would be able to do a better job with the carving.

Perhaps something unexpected had happened to Saijirô. He was always telling Oichi that he had a strong constitution, but he wasn't invincible, after all. He might have fallen ill and be lying in bed. It was also conceivable he had gone out scouting locations for her and had gotten caught up in the riot in Ueno the other day. *Highly unlikely!* Oichi scoffed at herself for being so naïve. Busy as he was, the last thing Saijirô would do would be to traipse around looking for places for her to draw. But even for the great "Silky Strand Saiji," her series of one hundred prints must have been his first big commission. To a carver, the way one depicted rain soaking a woman's hair was completely different to the rain shrouding the waters of the Sumida River. She couldn't rule out the possibility that he had gone out to scout locations.

Oichi put the lid back on the box containing her inkstone. She stood up thinking she would go over and look in on Saijirô, but then she thought better of it. Saijirô was not only the husband of Onobu but also the father of a small girl named Okayo. Lately this fact had assailed Oichi's senses like the smell of Saijirô own body. Oichi frowned. Of course she acknowledged that Saijirô had a wife and child, but she had never thought of him as a husband or a father. Why did she feel that there was such a difference between knowing he was married and thinking of him as the husband of some woman she had never met?

What should I do? Oichi didn't want to see Saijirô in his role as husband. Or rather, it wasn't so much that she didn't want to see him, but that it made her angry to think of him spending time at home together with the woman he had once claimed to have broken up with.

Oichi slipped on her sandals, which she had left on the step inside the front door. Saijirô's workshop was in Muramatsuchô. A cold wind whipped past Oichi as she crossed Ryôgoku Bridge. She passed several people carrying cloth bundles with straw ropes and bits of fern used for New Year decorations poking out. Then she remembered it was the year-end market at Sensôji Temple in Asakusa. Passing through Yone-zawachô lined with the residences of petty bureaucrats, she emerged onto a small side street behind Muramatsuchô.

As she began crossing the street, Oichi noticed a woman walking toward her from the direction of the Hamachô moat. She was a stocky woman with square shoulders and wore a rather unbecoming striped kimono. She was carrying a cloth bundle as though just returning from the year-end market. She was staring at Oichi.

Oichi stopped.

The woman also came to a halt in front of a paperhanger's shop. Next door to the paperhanger's was Saijirô's workshop. Oichi knew instinctively who the woman was. She was the last person in the world Oichi wanted to meet. The woman seemed to know who Oichi was, too. Oichi decided she would walk right on past Saijirô's workshop. After all, there was no reason why an artist such as herself shouldn't be seen walking about Muramatsuchô. But her body wouldn't move.

Onobu bowed politely to her. "It's nice of you to come by." Her face was wreathed in a smile. "Thank you for all you've done for my husband."

"Not at all, it's I who should be grateful." It was all Oichi could manage just to smile back at her.

Now that she had run into Onobu there was no turning back, she told herself. She had nothing to feel guilty about. If this woman hadn't had a child, Oichi herself would be Saijirô's wife. There was no reason she should feel tense or her voice should tremble.

"Please come inside." Onobu slid open the lattice door.

There's no turning back now, Oichi again told herself. She had been invited inside, so she would just have to go in and have a look around. Oichi went into the house. The entrance was at the side of the workshop. As Oichi stepped up onto the wooden floor of the hall there was a narrow staircase to her left.

"Please," Onobu said to Oichi, pointing to the stairs. At the same time, she slid back the shoji to the workshop and called in to Saijirô, "Someone to see you."

Oichi heard Saijirô's voice from inside the workshop, "Who is it?"

"Miss Yoshihana."

Oichi tried to imagine the look on Saijirô's face. But Onobu was still smiling when she turned around to speak to Oichi. "I'm afraid you'll find it very cramped," she said, leading the way up to the second floor.

The wooden floor of the upstairs corridor was polished to a high sheen. On the left was a veranda for drying clothes and on the right a six-mat room. On the other side of that there appeared to be another three-mat room.

"Please forgive the mess," said Onobu, sliding the door shut.

It appeared Onobu's daughter had been playing in the room with one of her friends. Scattered over the tatami was a crude paper doll that looked to have been crafted by childish hands, some colored paper, a pair of scissors, and a pot of glue.

"Our daughter's hopelessly spoiled, I'm afraid—it's because my husband indulges her too much."

Onobu shrugged her square shoulders and put a cloth bundle onto a shelf. The large woman was surprisingly quick—before Oichi knew what had happened, Onobu had used some coals from the brazier to light a small hand-warmer and placed a bowl piled high with rice crackers in front of Oichi.

"Do you care for sweets?"

"Thank you, but . . ." mumbled Oichi as Onobu touched her finger to the iron kettle to see whether the water was still hot.

"I made some *oshiruko* yesterday. It turned out very well, so please try some, won't you? I'll go warm it up right now."

As she spoke she placed a perfectly brewed cup of tea—slightly sweet and not too hot—on the tatami in front of where Oichi was kneeling.

"While I'm at it, I'll go call my husband again. He should have come straight up—what can he be up to, I wonder?"

Flashing Oichi a friendly smile, Onobu headed back down the stairs. Immediately, Oichi heard her voice calling out to Saijirô, who at last reluctantly pulled himself away from his workshop. From the sound of his heavy footsteps coming up the stairs he couldn't have been happy that Oichi had come to call on him. As he reached the top of the stairs Oichi regarded him silently. Without making eye contact, he went over to the brazier. He crouched in front of it, balancing on the tips of his toes, and began raking the ashes with the fire tongs for no apparent reason.

"There was nothing I could do about it," Oichi lied to Saijirô, whose back was turned to her. "I didn't mean to come here—I just ran into your wife and she insisted on inviting me in."

"Not surprising, considering she lives here and she's always walking around the neighborhood," he replied sullenly, apparently having seen through Oichi's lie.

She ignored the comment. "Well, since I'm here, when are you going to take me out sketching?"

"Don't know."

"Last time I saw you, you said to expect you in four or five days."

"Things don't always go according to plan."

"I see . . ." Oichi's tone became cool. She turned away so she wouldn't have to look at his back. She sensed Saijirô was looking at her but she pretended not to notice.

"We'll go soon," he said. "I hadn't forgotten about it, you know."

"Soon?"

"What else can I say?" Saijirô's tone became sharper. Oichi looked at him but he had turned his back on her again.

"I must be going."

Saijirô didn't reply.

"Don't get scolded by your wife after I've gone."

"Onobu has never asked me about you even once."

Oichi was quiet.

"That's what's great about her," he continued. "When I come home late at night, she just puts out my bedding without pestering me about where I've been or who I've seen." Saijirô had probably meant this statement matter-of-factly but to Oichi it sounded as though he were boasting. There was the sound of footsteps on the stairs and a sweet smell wafted into the room. Onobu was bringing up the *oshiruko*.

"Sorry to have kept you waiting."

Onobu had stopped just below the top step and was peering into the room. She was smiling from ear to ear as before. Just as Oichi was thinking she would have to eat Onobu's *oshiruko* and pretend to enjoy it, she heard the sound of tiny feet coming up the stairs. It must be Saijirô's daughter, she thought, who has come home and been told by one of the men in the workshop that her parents are both upstairs.

"Papa!"

Okayo slipped past her mother and ran over to Saijirô. The girl threw herself onto his back with utter abandon, right in front of Oichi, and pressed her cheeks—cold from playing outside—against him to warm them.

"Aren't you going to greet our visitor?" Saijirô said, turning his head to look at Okayo.

In an instant, the Saijirô whom Oichi knew vanished. His was no longer the face of "Silky Strand Saiji," Oichi's lover, but of the father of this young girl.

"Excuse me," Oichi blurted out. "I just remembered some urgent business I have to attend to," she said, and dashed down the stairs. As she was leaving, she could have sworn that she saw a look of triumph flash across Onobu's cheerful face.

⟡

Oichi raced through the front door of her house. As soon as she was inside, she put on the sash she used to tie back the sleeves of her kimono when she worked.

The hell with him!

The words that had been echoing inside her head as she ran home from Muramatsuchô found their voice. "The hell with him—changing his daughter's diapers one minute and embracing his mistress the next!"

So what if she makes his bed for him when he comes home late! So what if she goes to the year-end market! So what if she makes oshiruko!

Oichi had not had Saijirô's child. She wasn't one to sit at home, wondering why he hadn't kept his promise to come see her. Things like year-end markets completely slipped her mind. She had never once made *oshiruko!* All she did was sit inside and draw pictures from dawn till dusk, and when she got hungry she ate simmered tofu.

"You'll regret it some day! There's only one Utagawa Yoshihana— only one Oichi—in all of Edo." Muttering to herself, Oichi sat down at her desk.

A sheet of thin Mino paper with her half-completed view of a back street in Kanda's Mikawachô neighborhood lay exactly as she had left it. On one side she had drawn a gate at the entrance to a street of row houses—bills posted on it advertising a masseur and a seamstress fluttered in the wind. On the other side, beneath the eaves of a broker's establishment, a man dressed like a house servant sat repairing a child's pair of stilts. It was a scene such as anyone living in Edo would have happened upon many a time.

The child's hand was resting on the servant's knee, eagerly waiting for him to finish his work. Suddenly a thought flashed through Oichi's mind: *That's me.* Oichi was always waiting for someone. She had been seven when her mother died. When evening came, her playmates' mothers would call them inside, but Oichi's own house remained dark. Afraid to go in, she would wait outside sketching in the dirt until Yohei came home.

Once, after the bell had sounded at six o'clock, the sun had set and her father had still not returned home so Oichi went as far as the Komadome Bridge to wait for him. At last she had caught sight of his blue cotton leggings reflected blurrily through her tears as he approached. The taciturn Yohei had been unable to comfort his daughter. Picking her up in his arms, the best he could manage was "I'm back now, aren't I?" Oichi clung to his collar, her face brushing against his cheek now covered with stubble where in the morning there had been only smoothly-shaven skin.

When they finished their simple dinner, Oichi would sit on her father's knee, drawing pictures of her playmates, of bugs she had gazed at with horror, of the weeds by the side of the road that never failed to fascinate her. Though Yohei never spoke, at such times he looked happy. Once he had put a picture she had drawn of him inside the breast of his kimono and kept it there like a lucky charm. Later she heard from one of Yohei's employees that he had gone around showing it off to everyone in his workshop.

Then came the day when Oichi had announced to Yohei that she wanted to be an artist. Far from discouraging her, her taciturn father had somehow persuaded Kagaya Kichiemon to get Utagawa Kuniyoshi himself—then at the height of his fame—to agree to take her on as a disciple. From then on, Oichi had been waiting for the day when Yohei would come to regard her as an accomplished artist.

She had slept and worked in the now disused upstairs room, next to the veranda used for hanging out clothes. She remembered how, frustrated with herself for not being able to draw as well as she wished, she had deliberately stepped outside into the freezing cold wearing only a thin robe. And she could not even begin to count the number of times she had gotten out of bed unable to sleep for thinking about a picture she had been having trouble with, and had ended up staying up all night working on it.

It was around that time that Yohei—once a fussy eater given to complaining that Oichi used kindling instead of proper firewood for cooking—became indifferent to food. And even though he had never touched a sewing box in his life, she once witnessed him trying to thread a needle. Nevertheless, even if Oichi had stayed up late at night working she would always get up before Yohei left for work at six o'clock each morning. On days when he was working down at the kilns on the banks of the Genmori Canal where they fired the roof tiles, he would ask her to deliver his lunchbox to him at midday.

Yohei must have been aware that Oichi aspired to be the equal of the master roof tiler whom everyone called "the Clam." No doubt he—just as much as she—was looking forward to the day when he would be able to say to her, "My, you've outdone yourself, haven't you?"

Life with Yohei had been fun, with never a dull moment. But Oichi had been living under a delusion. She thought that since she had enjoyed living with Yohei, she would also be able to live happily ever after with Saijirô too. After all, hadn't he looked at her pictures and declared, "I'll make this my best work ever!"? Hadn't Yohei also been under the misapprehension that Saijirô, smitten as he was by Oichi's handiwork, would make her his wife? That was probably why several days before his death, Yohei, realizing his mistake, had vented his frustration to Kichiemon.

Now Oichi understood. What Saijirô needed wasn't Oichi to inspire him to prove how great he was as he wielded his chisel over a block of wood. No, what he needed was Onobu to silently put out his bedding for him when he came home late at night. No matter how long she waited, Saijirô would not come. And if he did come, he would only try to console her saying, "I'll see what I can do," before heading off again, having eased his guilty conscience.

You'll regret it some day!

There was only one Utagawa Yoshihana in Edo. No other artist could so delight Kichiemon that he would rush over to Saijirô's workshop shouting, "Carve this right away!"

The sash that Oichi had used to tie back her sleeves was beginning to cut into her arms. As she loosened it, the tolling of the temple bell in the cold night pierced the silence. The drawing of Mikawachô lying on her desk started to look blurred. Oichi turned away so her tears wouldn't spoil her picture.

VI

THE BUDDING TREE

Okaji was seated behind the lattice screen in the office of her restaurant going over the accounts on her abacus when the waitress, Ohatsu, suddenly appeared out of the corner of her eye.

She's probably come to get the blue-and-white porcelain saké pot, thought Okaji.

Okaji's restaurant, the Moegi, had a small office off to one side of the kitchen, separated from it by a raised wooden floor. The restaurant itself was not so large, and there was only one small standing cupboard used for storing dishes. Items such as large serving bowls and platters—as well as Okaji's prized blue-and-white porcelain saké pot—were kept on a shelf at the back of the office for lack of any better place to put them.

Once, one of the Moegi's regular customers had happened to poke his head into Okaji's office and been strangely taken by this rather unorthodox practice. The customer had pointed to the blue-and-white porcelain saké pot and asked that it be brought to his table. From then on, most of the Moegi's regular customers had started requesting to be served with such-and-such a dish or this-or-that saké flask. Okaji had obliged. The Moegi had by now quite a number of dishes reserved exclusively for their most valued customers.

Sometimes Okaji went so far as to buy slightly more expensive dishes to suit the individual tastes of specific patrons. Like the shelf itself, this too had been a case of necessity being the mother of invention: Okaji had grown tired of her customers poking their noses into her office whenever they felt like it. As it turned out, it tickled the vanity of the Moegi's patrons to know that when they came they would be served on dishes reserved for their own private use. Even in the summertime, when it was hot and people gravitated to restaurants along the Sumida River where they could sit and enjoy a cooling breeze, Okaji's customers made a point of coming to her out-of-the-way restaurant some distance from the waterfront.

But instead of walking over to the shelf to get the saké pot as Okaji had expected, Ohatsu knelt on the floor in front of her mistress.

"Um . . ."began Ohatsu. It appeared that she had come to announce that Okaji had a visitor.

Okaji tilted her head to one side and looked inquiringly at Ohatsu. Even though the waitress had not said who the visitor was, Okaji had a good idea. She was quite certain it was her ex-husband, Kumezô.

"Um . . ." repeated Ohatsu, still at a loss for words. At last she uttered the words Okaji had expected to hear, "The master of the Sansuitei is here to see you. I showed him to the upstairs room in back."

"I see . . ." Okaji closed her eyes and pressed the tips of her fingers against her temples.

In 1829, as the thirteenth year of the Bunsei era was drawing to a close amid a series of natural disasters, the government had attempted to improve the country's fortunes by changing the era name to Tenpô— but to no avail. In the five years since then, continued crop failures had triggered devastating famines throughout northeastern Japan, from Mutsu and Dewa provinces down through the northern Kantô region. In Edo the price of rice had shot up. In normal times, a hundred *mon* had bought twelve or thirteen *gô* of rice. This year in June it hit an all-time high—now the same amount of money bought just four and a half *gô*. As though trying to keep up, other commodities such as saké, soy sauce, and salt had also become much more expensive. Okaji was getting a headache simply going over the restaurant's accounts on her abacus.

And now Kumezô had come to see her. His own restaurant, the Sansuitei, was located east of the river in Mukôjima. Rumor had it that the Sansuitei—once a famous haunt of writers and artists—had been steadily losing customers over the past four or five years, apparently due to the scandalous behavior of the woman Kumezô had installed as his second wife. Kumezô wasn't capable of propping up his failing business, nor did it help matters that everywhere one turned these days all people were talking about was the famine. In Edo, incomes had not kept pace with inflation. Increasing numbers of people were finding that no matter how hard they worked they couldn't even afford to buy rice. To make matters worse, everyday hordes of refugees more dead than alive had been pouring into Edo from the worst famine-affected areas. The starving masses had begun turning their attention to the warehouses of merchants, who they suspected of hoarding supplies.

During the Tenmei famine fourteen or fifteen years earlier, some eight thousand businesses—liquor shops, pawnbrokers, and nearly a thousand rice stores—had been looted in massive riots. The government had learned its lesson. This time around officials were ordering wholesalers to release rice from their warehouses. By distributing relief supplies and setting up soup kitchens, the government had so far managed to keep the lid on an explosive situation. Even rich merchants seemed to be attuned to public sentiment—in an effort to forestall looting, they had taken to doling out free rice porridge outside their shops.

In short, it was no time for businessmen to be seen entertaining their clients at fancy restaurants like the Sansuitei. If Kumezô was coming to see Okaji at such a time, it could only mean one thing: he needed to borrow money.

But truth be told, Okaji's own restaurant was not doing all that well either. The Moegi had never been the sort of establishment that drew large groups of diners like guild associations or comedy clubs. It was the type of restaurant where loyal patrons dropped by on the spur of the moment and asked the chef to whip them up something good. And, perhaps for that very reason, business was as strong as ever. Nevertheless, Okaji was finding it increasingly difficult to get hold of good ingredients and was forced to spend more and more money in order to do so. Often the more customers she served the harder it was to break even.

"Nothing but headaches!" Okaji, having lost track of her calculations, tilted her abacus forward to line all the beads up in a row. Tapping her fingers against her forehead she stood up. Suddenly, from the direction of the front door, she heard a woman's scream. It sounded like Ohatsu. Okaji dashed out of her office into the corridor. Out of the corner of her eye, she saw the cook, Shinshichi, who had just finished sharpening and rinsing off a large cutting knife, step outside the back door. Okaji raced down the corridor, almost running into Omiyo, the maid, who had just come down the stairs. She stepped from the hallway down onto the earthen floor inside the front door. "Uhei, get hold of yourself! Please, Uhei!" she heard Ohatsu cry out, with tears in her voice. Okaji slid open the lattice door and was about to dash outside in her stocking feet when suddenly she froze.

Ohatsu was standing amid a circle of ghosts—or so it appeared. Shrouded in darkness, the wraithlike figures crouched on the ground, stretching out their bony arms toward her. Once Okaji had had time to collect herself, she realized that what she was seeing were in fact real people. They were collapsed on the ground around Ohatsu dressed in mud-spattered clothing—no more than rags, really—and had wasted away to skin and bones. What Okaji had taken for a cloak of darkness was merely the shadow of the Moegi's upper story.

"Please, Uhei!" sobbed Ohatsu, falling to her knees. Before her a man of about forty lay sprawled on the ground like a dead branch snapped off by the wind. Okaji suddenly remembered that Ohatsu had a cousin named Uhei who lived up north in Matsuida, in Jôshû province.

"Omiyo!" called out Okaji to the young maid, who was standing at the bottom of the stairs in a daze. At the sound of her name, Omiyo's body began to move as though of its own accord.

Scolding Ohatsu, Okaji helped the man up and instructed Omiyo to call for a doctor. Glancing around her, she saw Shinshichi trying to help an elderly lady who was too feeble to stand up on her own. Beside her was an old man who looked to be her companion and a child of thirteen or fourteen, both lying face down on the ground. There was also a younger woman with an infant on her back and another child of eleven or twelve, both of whom stared at Okaji with vacant, expressionless faces. It would appear that Ohatsu's cousin from Jôshû had come to Edo seeking her help with his parents, his wife, and three young children in tow.

_⌒⌒_

Though Kumezô was the last man Okaji had wanted to see, she had to admit that he turned out to be much more useful than Omiyo.

He had taken over from the maid after she retreated to the kitchen—apparently horrified at the abject state of Uhei and his family—and helped them change out of their dirty, sweaty clothes into some lightweight cotton robes that Okaji managed to scrape together from her clothes chests. He even helped feed Uhei's elderly parents the rice porridge that Shinshichi hastily prepared.

Afterward, Okaji invited Kumezô into her office and offered him a drink. Though she only meant it as a small token of her appreciation, he seemed to get the wrong idea, thinking that now all was forgiven and forgotten between them. He sat cross-legged on the floor instead of kneeling, and started helping himself to the saké without waiting for Okaji to pour it. At some point, he switched from addressing her politely as "Okaji-san" and began referring to her instead as plain old "Okaji." To top it all off, from time to time he casually rested his hand on Okaji's shoulder, as though he thought that any woman ought to be flattered by his advances. Ever so subtly, Okaji drew away.

Kumezô was in a talkative mood. Perhaps he remembered how Okaji had once told him, long ago, that she liked the sound of his voice so much it sent shivers down her spine—now she noticed it had a nasally twang and she wondered why it had ever appealed to her.

Shinshichi brought over a small bowl of sliced squid pickled in salt—something he never served to the Moegi's customers but prepared purely for his own consumption for when he drank saké. Kumezô, spurning the chopsticks, picked some up with his fingers and tossed it into his mouth. "Mmm . . . delicious!" he exclaimed, closing his eyes in delight.

Okaji was by now bored of her tête-à-tête with Kumezô. Surreptitiously, she motioned to Shinshichi to join them. He seemed to have had the same idea, for he had brought his own teacup over with him from the kitchen. Glancing quickly at Kumezô, he stepped up onto the raised floor of the accounting office.

Kumezô looked taken aback. He seemed to have been expecting Okaji to order Shinshichi back to the kitchen with a peremptory "Can't you see we're talking?" Instead, she refreshed the leaves in the pot and poured Shinshichi a cup of tea.

Kumezô looked at Okaji, then at Shinshichi. Despite his high-handed manner, he was a man whose confidence was easily shaken. It was only then that it seemed to occur to him that Okaji's feelings for him were not what they had been ten years before.

"Having tea, are you?" he remarked to Shinshichi to cover his embarrassment. "You don't drink during the day, is that it? Well, you're a better man than I am." Shrugging his shoulders, Kumezô picked up the saké pot and shook it to demonstrate that it was empty. Shinshichi's kitchen apprentice, Shôkichi, brought over the kettle used for warming saké. Shinshichi took it from him and replenished the saké pot on the table.

"So what happened with that man who was sprawled on the ground outside?" Kumezô resumed the conversation. "There wasn't anything actually wrong with him, was there?" he asked Shinshichi.

It was Shinshichi who had taken the doctor home after he had examined Uhei and his family. His only response to Kumezô's question, however, was to nod his head and take another sip of tea. Having broken up Okaji and Kumezô's tête-à-tête, the cook, taciturn by nature, seemed at a loss for words.

"The doctor was of the opinion that he had just fainted from hunger and fatigue," said Okaji, answering for Shinshichi when she saw that Kumezô was waiting for an answer. "He should get his strength back as long as he keeps eating porridge."

"And until then you plan to let him sleep in that room?"

"Well, I suppose so," replied Okaji with a pained smile.

Uhei and his family were installed in the Moegi's downstairs room, which was very popular with the restaurant's patrons on account of its fine bamboo-trimmed alcove. Three days ago a customer had sent a messenger round to reserve the room for six o'clock that evening. A little while earlier Okaji had dispatched Omiyo to explain the situation but instead of offering to take one of the upstairs rooms instead, the man sent back word saying that he wished to change his reservation to another day. Yet another customer had arrived during all the confusion and had gone home. Under the circumstances, Okaji was in no position to tell Ohatsu and her cousin that his family could stay there as long as they wanted.

"Well, it's the perfect time then," said Kumezô, looking away from Okaji.

Okaji studied Kumezô carefully. "What do you mean, the perfect time?" she asked.

Kumezô paused before answering. He seemed to be studying Okaji's expression. "To come back to the Sansuitei," he said at last.

"Don't be ridiculous!" Okaji replied, turning away in surprise. After all, she pointed out to Kumezô, wasn't it he who had forced her to leave in the first place when he had brought home that woman he had gotten pregnant?

"I know, I know," responded Kumezô weakly. "Everything is my fault. If I'd been stronger, none of this would have happened."

Shinshichi sipped his tea.

Kumezô continued, "But I expect you know that my mother died and that that woman left me for another man." This last bit of information was news to Okaji. "Come back, Okaji. Now that you can't use that room, this is the perfect chance."

"You've got some nerve saying that now."

"At this point, I don't care what people think anymore." Kumezô glanced at Shinshichi, who kept his eyes lowered as he sipped his tea. "I can't go on like this," he continued. "I'll be forced to kill myself—and my children too."

"Well, you've dug your own grave," responded Okaji.

"How can you be so cold?" shot back Kumezô in his soft, nasal voice. Okaji looked away. "I didn't know you could be so cruel, Okaji." Kumezô sighed deeply. "I tell you all my problems, and all you can do is get upset."

Okaji looked at Shinshichi. It had been impulsive of her to bring the cook over to join them. She realized that now. So this is the sort of man that Okaji was married to, he must have been thinking to himself.

More desperate now than before, Kumezô continued, throwing aside all restraint. "As a matter of fact, Okaji, I'm broke. I came here today to borrow money from you."

"Is that so?"

"*Is that so?*—Is that all you can say? Don't you realize I'll lose the Sansuitei?"

"What do you mean?"

"It's mortgaged to the hilt." For no apparent reason, a smile appeared on Kumezô's handsome features. "If I don't pay the interest I owe in ten days, the Sansuitei will pass out of our family's hands forever."

"But I'm not a member of your family any longer, now am I?"

"Not family! So that's how you feel, is it?" Kumezô's smile broadened. "I'm begging you, Okaji. Thirty *ryô* will do."

"Thirty *ryô*? Where do you think I'd come up with that kind of money? This isn't the Sansuitei, you know. We barely manage to scrape by one day at a time."

"Even scraping by one day at a time, by now you must have put aside a lot of money."

"No, I haven't."

Kumezô again glanced at Shinshichi. "If that's the case, then come back to the Sansuitei—just for a little while." Kumezô looked at Okaji, then at Shinshichi. The latter continued quietly sipping his tea. "I know someone who's willing to lend me money provided you come back."

"Absolutely not." Okaji shook her head vigorously. "I've got enough on my hands with the Moegi alone. We're just starting to make a name for ourselves."

"But still, it's nothing compared to the Sansuitei . . ."

As much as it pained Okaji to admit it, Kumezô was right.

Okaji was the daughter of a saké dealer in Honjo's Yokoamichô district. When her neighbors learned she was to be adopted by Hikobei, the owner of Mukôjima's famous Sansuitei restaurant, they had all been astonished. It was considered a big step up in the world for Okaji and her family.

Of course, Hikobei—who was distantly related to Okaji's father—had not chosen Okaji on a whim. He had made careful inquiries about her reputation before going to Yokoamichô with a proposal. Okaji's father was a very easygoing man in all respects, and had responded simply by saying that now he thought about it, he *did* vaguely recall having distant relatives in Mukôjima. And with that, the matter was settled.

Okaji married Kumezô the following year. She was sixteen; he was twenty. Kumezô was the nephew of Hikobei's wife, Oriku, the second son of her elder sister, whose husband owned a cotton business on Hirokôji in Ueno. Since Hikobei had no siblings or children of his own, under normal circumstances one would expect him to have adopted Kumezô and choose a bride for him. But the young man was wayward by nature and had already backed out of one engagement after everything had already been settled.

Nevertheless, Oriku doted on her handsome nephew, who all the young women in the neighborhood said resembled this or that kabuki actor, or was a modern-day Prince Genji, or whatnot. So when her husband decided to adopt Okaji, Oriku asked him to let Kumezô marry her. Initially Hikobei had been unwilling to entertain the idea. But when his wife had clasped her hands beseechingly and begged, "Please, I'll never ask you another favor!" Hikobei had reluctantly given in.

What had really clinched the matter, however, was that the sixteen-year-old Okaji had fallen head over heels in love with Kumezô. As far as she was concerned, his waywardness was the result of his being too nice to rebuff the advances of all the young women who threw themselves at him. And even if he *had* led a somewhat dissolute life so far, she was sure that he would settle down once he was married.

Oriku, for her part, was in the habit of saying that everyone knew all restaurant owners were playboys. After all, the success or failure of a restaurant depended on three things: its cook, its waitresses, and its matron. The more attention a wife paid to running her restaurant, the more likely her husband was to fool around. Hikobei himself had been quite the rake in his youth. There had even been an incident once where his mistress had come barging into the Sansuitei with his illegitimate children in tow.

The year after seeing Kumezô and Okaji safely wed, Hikobei had died. There was now nothing to hold Kumezô's waywardness in check.

Despite his scandalous behavior, there was no denying that Hikobei had been a talented restaurateur: he had remodeled the Sansuitei in an appealing, rustic manner and kept a close eye on the food, being no mean hand himself in the kitchen. Kumezô, in contrast, had nothing to offer other than his extraordinary good looks. It wasn't as if he had a head for numbers, nor was he any judge of what tasted good and what didn't.

Over time, Okaji grew to dislike Kumezô. As she gradually came to realize that there was nothing behind his clean-cut good looks, even his confident smile began to make her cringe. There also was something slightly unclean about him, as though the sweat and face powder of other women had penetrated his skin.

One day, after Kumezô had stayed out two nights in a row without offering any explanation when he finally returned home, Okaji had dragged her futon upstairs rather than sleep in the same room with him. Through all of this, Oriku never reproached her nephew. It seemed she had finally found a release for all her pent-up frustration and resentment in watching her adopted daughter taste the same suffering that had been visited on her by Hikobei over the years.

Then, soon after the rites marking the third anniversary of Hikobei's death, Kumezô came home with a woman whose belly was noticeably swollen. *He's brought her here at last!* Okaji thought to herself. She had long been aware that Kumezô kept a mistress in a little village east of the river called Yanagishima. She even knew that the woman's name was Omura. And she had found out that Oriku had been secretly sending her an allowance.

Without so much as a word, Okaji handed her husband's mistress a large sum of money and sent her back to Yanagishima to have the baby, with the understanding that afterward Omura would return with the child to her parents' house in Zôshigaya.

But some three months later Omura appeared again at the Sansuitei, this time with a plump child in her arms. It turned out that Oriku had sent for her.

"Well, after all, *you* haven't given me a grandchild," Oriku said by way of explanation. To this, Okaji had no reply. And so Omura took up residence at the Sansuitei. Even Oriku, apparently, had not planned to actually take her in but when Omura broke down in tears and said she'd rather die than be parted from her child, Oriku's heart immediately went out to her.

Once she was settled in, Omura deferred to Oriku in everything. She would ask Oriku's permission before so much as buying a toy for her child. By contrast, Okaji never sent the waitresses to Oriku when they had a problem but instead handled the matter herself. Or, if Oriku informed her that a customer was asking to see "the young madam," Okaji never brushed it aside as mere flattery but ran off straight away to say hello. So it was no wonder Oriku found Omura more endearing. All she had to say to make Omura deliriously happy was, "Go ahead, buy the child a drum."

Oriku began inviting Omura to accompany her when she went to the theater. When the waitresses realized that Omura was in Oriku's good graces, they began to curry favor with her, and Omura's behavior became more and more brazen. If she was going to the theater but was short of cash, she would approach Okaji in her office as she pored over the accounts on her abacus and demand more.

Okaji opted to keep quiet and do as she was told. She had always thought it a mistake on her part to agree to let Hikobei adopt her. If she had come right out and told him she was happy being the daughter of a saké dealer and was not interested in becoming matron of the Sansuitei, then Hikobei would certainly have given in to Oriku's fervent plea and adopted Kumezô instead. And if Kumezô had been made heir to the Sansuitei, Oriku would have made sure that the person chosen to be his wife was someone more to her liking.

But there were limits even to what Okaji was willing to put up with. That limit was reached one summer about two years after Omura had come to live at the Sansuitei. Omura had left her toddling infant in the care of one of the waitresses and gone off to the theater with Oriku. Watching them alight from their palanquin upon their return,

Okaji suddenly became fed up with it all. Why was she slaving away and going without sleep simply so these two could live in comfort? Once she realized how miserable she was, the feeling would not go away. Okaji reproached herself for wanting to leave, saying she would be dishonoring Hikobei's memory by abandoning the Sansuitei. But everything around her seemed dirty, from the bedding soiled by Omura's child to the clothing Kumezô took off and threw on the floor. Carrying only a few personal belongings, Okaji left the Sansuitei. That had been ten years ago.

Her parents had long since closed up their saké business and moved in with their eldest son, who ran a hardware store in Aioichô. Though he urged her to come live with them, Okaji couldn't very well intrude on her brother, what with his family of five children to look after. Instead, she decided to take up employment at a restaurant in Takanawa.

Though Okaji had of course taken care to conceal both her real name and the fact that she was the former matron of the Sansuitei, about six months after she had begun working at the restaurant, a well-built man came to see her. It was Kumezô's older brother, Izaemon.

"I apologize for all the trouble my brother and my aunt have caused you," he said, prostrating himself on the tatami before her. "Please come back to the Sansuitei."

Apparently, Oriku had thought she would have no trouble running the Sansuitei all on her own, but she had forgotten that she was not her late husband. She had complained incessantly about the fish the chef ordered until the man, who had worked there for fifteen years, got fed up and left.

Izaemon sighed as he related the goings on since Okaji's departure. "I couldn't bear to stand by and watch any longer," he said. "I know I'm sticking my nose in where it doesn't belong, but since Uncle Hikobei was always so good to me while he was alive, I took it upon myself to come find you."

Hikobei had been good to her, too, thought Okaji. In the beginning, he had come to her defense if any of the waitresses, let alone the cook, made fun of her. "How dare you talk like that to my daughter!"

he would say, becoming truly upset. But Okaji had no desire to return to the Sansuitei. Even if she had, would Oriku really be willing to turn the office back over to Okaji, considering what a great job she thought she was doing of running the restaurant on her own?

"No, you're absolutely right," admitted Izaemon. He smiled ruefully to himself as he slid his hand inside the breast of his kimono. When he withdrew it, Okaji saw that his hand was causally clasping something wrapped in a piece of purple silk cloth. It was a bundle of coins. "May I loan you some money?" he said, looking directly at her.

Okaji thought she must have misheard. True, she was his brother's wife—but she was also the woman who had walked out on his brother and demanded a divorce. There was no reason on earth why he should want to loan her money.

"I brought this thinking I would give it to you if you agreed to come back to the Sansuitei," Izaemon explained. "But you're right. Even if you did, my aunt wouldn't let you in the house. So perhaps you could use this to open up your own restaurant." He was sure it would have made his uncle Hikobei very happy, Izaemon added.

In the end, after much wavering, Okaji accepted Izaemon's money. With it she was able to rent a shop in Kayachô and open the Moegi. It had been a stroke of good luck, and she had named it the Moegi—the "Budding Tree"—in the hope that it would also symbolize her new start in life.

That was not to say that the Moegi had been an instant success. The Sansuitei had done its best to interfere with her business. And it had been some time before she was able to find a good cook. The first one absconded with a large sum of money and Okaji had been forced to borrow more at an exorbitant rate. Unable to make the interest payments, she had once ended up at a teahouse with a loan shark, and another time found herself bowing and scraping before a group of gangsters who menacingly flaunted their tattoos as she begged for more time.

"I'll never go back to the Sansuitei—never!" Okaji muttered to herself as she stared off into the distance. Okaji loved her restaurant. The Moegi was her baby, the child she had given birth to and nurtured.

When fixing it up after first renting it, she had driven the carpenters to distraction with all her demands. Even after finding her current cook, Shinshichi, at first she had done nothing but criticize his cooking. "Too bland!" had been her continual complaint.

It was only after opening the Moegi that Okaji realized for the first time that she truly enjoyed working in the restaurant business. She hadn't stayed up late at night doing the accounts at the Sansuitei just so Oriku and Omura could live comfortably—she had done it simply because it was what she loved.

Okaji was grateful that the Moegi had given her the opportunity to indulge this love of hers. It may have been a cramped, insignificant little restaurant, but in Okaji's eyes the Moegi was more beautiful, more stylish, and more impressive than any other in Edo. She loved the stains on the walls where the young and impulsive Shinshichi, outraged that Okaji had dared to criticize his cooking, had hurled some dish of food or other. She loved the scratches on the lattice screen in her office left by a tattooed hoodlum who had brandished his dagger at her. She loved it all. And she was sure that Hikobei would have been delighted at the Moegi's success.

_◦◦◦_

"You want me to kill myself, is that it?" The sound of Kumezô's voice roused Okaji from her reverie. "Shall I start looking for a pine tree with a good stout limb to hang myself from?"

Okaji pictured Kumezô in a tattered cotton kimono wandering the banks of the Sumida River. A sour lump rose in the base of her throat and she suddenly felt unwell. "What was the name of the loan shark you borrowed money from?" she asked.

"That guy in Honjo who . . ." Kumezô paused in mid sentence and looked at Shinshichi. Then he drained his saké cup and abruptly drew himself up. "Well, never mind. I'll manage somehow."

"Are you sure?"

"Don't worry—I said I'll manage," he repeated, thumping his chest and casting a sidelong glance at Shinshichi, whose presence seemed to bother him. Then, just as Okaji was thinking that Kumezô still had some pride left, he added in a pathetic tone, "I may have made a complete mess of things, but there's always my big brother." Apparently Kumezô intended to ask Izaemon for help.

"Right, then," he said, reaching for the bowl of pickled squid as he rose from the table. After popping the last few pieces into his mouth he licked his fingers and wiped them on some tissue paper that he took from the breast of his kimono. "I guess I wasn't thinking straight. I should have known I couldn't leave you alone for ten years without you going and finding yourself another man."

For a moment Okaji didn't know whether she should reproach Kumezô for jumping to ridiculous conclusions or say something like, "Well, I see nothing gets past you!" and laugh off his remark. It was true Okaji had feelings for Shinshichi but the cook, for his part, had never so much as made a pass at her.

"Boy, I don't envy you," said Kumezô to Shinshichi as he left the room, adding, "Take care of your mistress—and those sick people in there."

"Sure."

From the other room they heard the sound of one of Uhei's elderly parents coughing.

⁓◦⦁◦⁓

Shinshichi's eyes beckoned to Okaji from across the room. She nodded silently, rose from her desk, and stepped down into the kitchen. She knew what it was he was going to tell her: he had been unable to purchase as much rice as she had hoped.

"Can you go talk to him?" the cook asked her.

One of the Moegi's regular customers was a rice wholesaler in Kuramae. Last night, Okaji had told Shinshichi that if necessary she would go to him for help. Now she was left with no choice. Okaji changed and got ready to go out.

There was no sign of Ohatsu as Okaji left the Moegi. But since things were quiet in the restaurant for the moment, she assumed the waitress must have gone to look in on Uhei and his family, who had recently moved to a tenement on a back street in Suwachô.

Okaji spotted Ohatsu standing waiting for her outside the gate of the local Gion shrine—the "Dumpling God Shrine" as it was popularly known. Every year in mid-July, during the Gion Festival, the shrine's parishioners left rice dumplings stuck on sprigs of bamboo grass as offerings to the god Gozu. Worshippers to the shrine would take these home believing they had the power to ward off evil spirits. Though it was still early in the month, already the grounds of the shrine were thronged with people who were no doubt there to pray to the god to put an end to that year's crop failures and rampant price inflation.

"Please, ma'am. Could you spare a moment?" said Ohatsu, taking Okaji forcefully by the hand and leading her around behind the shrine. Though the ground in back was usually dank and muddy, the dark soil had become parched and cracked from the drought that had set in during June.

"I wonder if you could give my cousin—Uhei, that is—a job, ma'am?"

"Uhei?" Okaji frowned—and for good reason.

Uhei and his family had spent five days at the Moegi. At noon on the sixth day they had left for the tenement in Suwachô that Ohatsu had found for them. The entire family—Uhei, his wife, his elderly parents, his small children, and Ohatsu herself—had gathered to say goodbye to Okaji, thanking her for all she had done for them.

For her part, Okaji was glad to have been of service, and she preferred not to say anything to Ohatsu about the days leading up to the family's departure. But truth be told, once they had recovered their strength, Uhei, his wife, and their two small children had consumed an astonishing amount of food. By the time they left, all the extra rice Okaji had stocked up on was gone.

"Please, ma'am, won't you give Uhei a job just to help him out? We haven't been able to find work for him anywhere."

Her first thought, Ohatsu explained, was that Uhei and his older boy, Senta, could find work as salt peddlers. A salt dealer would lend them everything they needed— measuring cups, buckets, and a carrying pole to sling over their shoulders—and even give them the merchandise on credit and let them settle up once they had sold it. It was the easiest trade there was to get started in. However, she had taken them to two different salt dealers only to be turned away, both saying they didn't need any help at the moment.

Uhei and his family were not the only people from up north to come to Edo seeking help from siblings or cousins in the big city. Once they arrived they had to find work, and since peddling salt didn't require any money to get started, it was invariably the first occupation people turned to. The salt dealers Ohatsu had visited said they didn't even have any poles left to lend them.

Ohatsu's other attempts to find work—for Uhei as a menial worker at a pawnbroker's and for Senta as a delivery boy at a soba restaurant—had met with similar failure. Even a plasterer and a roof-tiler had turned them down.

"So that's what happened," said Ohatsu, concluding her story. "You see, ma'am, you're the only person now who can help us."

"You say I can help, but the Moegi is hardly without its own problems."

"I know that, ma'am. I know—but Uhei's parents looked after me when I was young, so I have to try to help them."

"Yes, you mentioned that once."

"They're decent people—they really are. After all they've done for me, I can't bear to see my aunt and uncle and my cousin and his family living like this." Ohatsu, still holding Okaji's hand in hers, wiped a tear from her cheek with the other.

She told Okaji the only reason Uhei and his family had not starved to death already was that they went morning, noon, and night to eat at the makeshift soup kitchens set up around Edo which doled out rice gruel. Even so, the family was glad that they had come to Edo, Ohatsu said. Up north, when the famine first started, they had eaten the seed for the following year's rice crop. Then, when that was gone, they would eat anything they could get their hands on: a bit of straw if they were lucky, but usually mud dumplings. In Edo, even if they only slept on reed mats laid down over a dirt floor, at least there was a roof over their heads and rice gruel to eat. Compared to life up north, the city seemed like paradise to them.

"But there is one problem," continued Ohatsu. "The people next door to them in Suwachô make miso soup every morning, and in the evening they take an earthenware cooking stove outside to the back alley and grill dried fish. How would you like it if you had to smell such delicacies being prepared day in and day out? Don't you think you'd get fed up with eating rice gruel, lucky as you are to have it?"

"I guess I would," admitted Okaji.

"There's plenty of fish and miso to be had in Edo—provided you've got the means to buy it."

The money Okaji had given Uhei's family that day when they left the Moegi had disappeared on used clothing for Ohatsu's aunt and uncle. The little bit of cash Ohatsu had given them herself was barely enough to buy straw sandals and tissue paper to wipe their noses. The children had no change of clothes at all. Each evening they had to bathe at the neighborhood well behind the house, subjected to the sight of the fish being grilled next door. It had finally become too much—the other day the children had raided the cooking stove when the neighbor's wife stepped inside for a moment.

"Uhei and I both gave them a good scolding but my heart went out to the poor dears." Now you see how it is, won't you please help them? Ohatsu implored Okaji, squeezing her hand so hard it hurt. "Think of it as charity if you like, ma'am. But please give Uhei a job."

"I feel terribly sorry for them—I really do." With the recent run up in prices, Okaji explained, now was not the time to take on new staff. She already employed three people in the kitchen: her cook Shinshichi and his assistants Shôkichi and Asaji. She would have liked to hire one more waitress but it would eat up all her profits.

"Don't say that, ma'am. If you can't hire Uhei, then how about Ogen, his wife? I know you wouldn't want her to wait on guests, but she could clear tables and do the cleaning. You could give her half—no, just a quarter of her wages in advance. How about it, ma'am? Please!"

Okaji was no match for Ohatsu. She paid her waitresses between three and three and a half *ryô* a year, but for clearing tables and other odd jobs two and half *ryô* would suffice. One-quarter of that came to ten *shu*. Okaji figured she could manage that much. And even if she weren't to hire Ogen, she still couldn't just ignore Ohatsu's plea for help. She would probably end up giving her that much anyway, either in the form of cash or second-hand clothes.

"Alright, I'll do it. But in return I'll need a little more time to pay her advance wages."

"Oh, thank you!" Ohatsu bowed deeply, all but falling to her knees and prostrating herself on the ground. "I'll go tell my cousin straight away!" She scampered off without so much as looking back, probably hoping to get away before Okaji changed her mind. Behind her, pale clouds of dust rose up from the parched, cracked earth.

Okaji covered her mouth with the end of her sleeve and let out a sigh. She had just remembered why it was she had come out: to ask a man to sell her some rice, even if she had to pay a bit more than usual for it.

—⚬⚬—

"Excellent—the best meal I've eaten in ages!" said Kichiemon, proprietor of the Kagaya bookstore in Ryôgoku's Yonezawachô district, as a smile of deep satisfaction spread across his fat, droopy cheeks. "Even so," he continued, "things are tough these days. You must have trouble even finding something so basic as a bit of ginger root."

"That's true. But after all, we *are* in the business of providing good things for our customers to eat."

"Indeed."

Okaji nudged a tray of as yet untouched sweets toward Kichiemon as Ohatsu poured him the tea.

After learning her lesson the previous month when the Moegi had run out of rice, Okaji had gone to Kameido, a small village east of the river, to find a farmer who would agree to sell directly to her. At first she got nowhere. Some farmers, as soon as they saw she was a woman, would quote her an exorbitant price, while others said they already had contracts with other restaurants. But on the third day, she had chanced across a kindly farmer who had agreed. All the vegetables served at the Moegi that day had been delivered directly from his farm.

"Well, I think I'll be going then," Kichiemon said, his fat body quivering as he rose from the table. Ohatsu slid open the fusuma doors and Kichiemon passed through, ducking slightly out of force of habit even though his head cleared the lintel by a good three or four inches.

At the entrance to the restaurant, Omiyo neatly placed his sandals side by side atop the stone on the earthen floor inside the front door. As he bantered away with the waitress, Kichiemon balanced precariously on one foot while reaching out for a sandal with the other. His feet were surprisingly small for someone his size, and the strain of his enormous frame—which easily weighed two hundred and fifty pounds—was evidently too much. He lurched to one side, lost his balance, and began to topple over.

Ohatsu and Omiyo, standing below him on the earthen floor having already put on their sandals, rushed to Kichiemon's side just in time to catch him before he fell all the way over. He smiled an embarrassed smile, his squinty eyes narrowing to mere slits. Then he brushed the dirt from the soles of his tabi, put on his sandals, and went out through the lattice doorway. Watching him, Okaji thought he looked a bit unsteady on his feet and offered to call him a palanquin. Kichiemon declined, saying he didn't have far to go, and Okaji sent Ohatsu along with him instead. "If I fall over again, you must put your arms around me and lift me up," he quipped jovially to Ohatsu.

Okaji returned to her office with a smile still on her lips. There, she found Shinshichi and Asaji standing side-by-side waiting for her. From the looks on their faces, neither of *them* was in a particularly jovial mood.

"Not again?"

Asaji nodded and put an empty basket on the table in front of her. It should have been full of eggs.

"What are we going to do?" Okaji frowned.

Uhei's wife had been working at the Moegi for two months now. Though Ohatsu had advertised Ogen as a hard worker, she was accident prone and had done such things as splash water on the ink painting hanging in the decorative alcove while mopping the floor, or get lost while out on an errand and return empty handed, forcing Okaji to send Omiyo out again later. "Ever since she arrived, Ogen's made my job harder, not easier!" Omiyo had complained bitterly several times already.

"No doubt when it comes to farm work, Ogen is three or four times faster than either of us," Okaji said, trying to placate Omiyo. "But she hasn't got the hang of working in a restaurant yet. When she does, I'm sure she'll go around cleaning this place just a quickly as if she was clearing a field."

This is what Okaji had told herself when she had discovered the ruined ink painting, and had taken a deep breath rather than scolding Ogen for her carelessness. Then a month ago, Ogen had sent Ohatsu to ask Okaji for another advance on her wages. "Not on your life!" Okaji had exclaimed, unable to control her emotions any longer. This is the thanks I get for keeping quiet up 'til now, she thought.

Okaji didn't know exactly how Ohatsu broke the news to Ogen that Okaji wouldn't lend her any more money, but the next day Ogen had apparently been griping to Omiyo about it while the two were doing the cleaning. "How far does the missus think eight *shu* goes, anyway?" In fact, Okaji knew better than Ogen how quickly money slipped through one's fingers. "The restaurant's customers are paying one or two *shu* per head," Ogen was also heard to say, "so how is it the missus can't spare eight *shu* to lend me?" What Ogen didn't know was that to put two *shu* worth of food on the table, almost as much went out the door in the process of preparing it.

Yet Ogen was right to complain that one couldn't support a family of seven on eight *shu*. However much Ogen may have wanted to prepare meals for her family, rice was simply too expensive. A hundred *mon* bought just four and a half *gô,* and to cook it she would also have to buy an iron kettle and firewood. If she wanted to make miso soup, then she would need to buy miso paste, tofu, and of course a cooking pot, an earthenware brazier, and charcoal. Ogen's eight *shu* would be gone before one could blink twice. Okaji knew all this. That was why she gave Ogen the restaurant's leftovers every day to take home with her. But lately Ogen had looked less pleased about this than she had at first.

It was about ten days before Kichiemon's visit that things had started to go missing. First, a small amount of money had vanished from Okaji's office. Then sweets and eggs had begun disappearing from the kitchen. Next it had been eggplants—and then eggs again.

Okaji was fairly certain the thefts were Ogen's handiwork. When she was done with the cleaning, Ogen invariably retreated to the small room beneath the stairs and hardly ever left it. But on each occasion when a theft had been discovered—and on those occasions only—

both Shinshichi and Asaji had observed Ogen entering either Okaji's office or the kitchen beforehand. And each time, without fail, Ogen would immediately leave the restaurant without saying where she was going, returning less than an hour later. Okaji suspected she slipped the things into the sleeves of her kimono and took them back home to her family in Suwachô.

"Please, ma'am," said Asaji. "It's high time you got rid of that woman. We're the ones who suffer every time Ogen steals something. It's not as though we have enough eggs in the first place. How can we get by if we lose five or six?"

"I'm sorry. Let's just be patient," Okaji said, massaging her temples feeling a headache coming on. "I'm still not convinced it's her who's stealing things."

"If not Ogen then who?" retorted Asaji.

"Look, I've been generous to Ogen—she has no need to steal, that's all."

"Then why don't you try asking her?" interrupted Shinshichi.

Massaging her temples again, Okaji nodded. Now was the perfect time to talk to Ogen. Ohatsu would certainly try to interfere if she were around, but she was out seeing Kichiemon home to Yonezawachô and probably wouldn't be back for more than an hour, after peeking in at the vaudeville theaters and listening to the monologues given at the sideshow huts along Hirokôji in Ryôgoku.

Okaji had forgotten to eat lunch but she didn't have much of an appetite, so when Shinshichi put a small bowl of pickled squid down in front of her she said she didn't want any. "Pour some green tea over it and eat it with some rice," he told her. She had just picked up her chopsticks and was about to begin eating when she heard the sound of the back gate opening. It seemed Ogen had returned.

"Want to speak to her later?" asked Shinshichi. Okaji shook her head, whereupon Asaji darted out of the kitchen and returned with Ogen.

Ogen kneeled in the doorway with her back slightly hunched, examining the striped kimono Okaji was wearing and the tray of food in front of her. Ogen had on an Echigo-weave linen kimono that Okaji had given her. It was badly crumpled from Ogen having tucked up the skirts and tied back her sleeves when she worked.

"Where have you been?" Okaji handed her teacup to Asaji who refilled it for her. As Okaji sipped her tea, Ogen, her face lowered, glanced quickly up at Okaji.

"To Suwachô—I had to go look in on the children."

"Forgive me if I'm mistaken, but the eggs that were in this basket—do you know what happened to them?"

Ogen stared at Okaji without saying a word. Okaji started to feel somewhat uncomfortable, even though she was the one who was asking the questions. She looked away and raised her teacup to her lips. Just then, Ogen spoke.

"I took them."

"Why, of all the nerve . . . !"

"Stop it!" shouted Okaji shrilly.

Before the words were even out of Okaji's mouth, Shinshichi had grabbed Asaji's arm just as he had been on the verge of striking Ogen. Asaji flailed about, trying to break free of Shinshichi's grip. "Please, ma'am, let me hit her, just once! I had to go running around Asakusa looking in every greengrocer's shop until I found some eggplants to replace the ones she stole!"

"And after all that effort, you still had more than you needed," spat out Ogen. "What a waste!"

"What do you mean?" Okaji asked.

"There are people in this world who have nothing but rice gruel to eat." said Ogen. "Even worse—some are eating balls of mud and straw. What a waste!" she repeated. "At first, I was happy to get the restaurant's leftovers. I'd never eaten such fine food in all my life and when I took it home my children were ecstatic—even with rice porridge to eat, they were almost always hungry. But then when I thought about it, I realized it meant that before I came along, you had so much of this fancy food you had to throw it away!"

"Now just a minute, Ogen!" Okaji put her teacup down on the tray in front of her. "You say we we're making fancy food while people are starving, but after all this is a business. If we didn't serve the best food we could, Shinshichi and Asaji and I wouldn't be able to make a living."

"Ma'am. You've never had to eat mud dumplings, have you?" asked Ogen, hunching over further. "You rinse the dirt in water several times just like you're washing rice and then you put it over the fire. Instead of being rough, the mud turns all gooey and sticky. Then you roll it into balls and eat it —they taste kind of salty. It's really not as bad as you might think."

Okaji said nothing.

Ogen continued. "Now, I don't know whether this is true or not, but I've heard that if you keep eating them the mud will build up in your tummy and eventually you'll die. Anyway, that's what we used to eat back up north."

"What are you trying to say—that we should make mud dumplings too?" screamed Asaji, bits of saliva flying from his mouth and his face flushed with anger. The only thing preventing him from raising his fist was Shinshichi's firm grip. "It's true," he continued, "while you were up north eating mud dumplings, I was here in Edo making fish dumplings. When I was an apprentice, I remember watching my master take those fish dumplings I'd made, pour a little broth over them, and scatter a few cherry blossom petals on top. I couldn't sleep after that, thinking about what sort of dishes I'd invent when *I* became a full-fledged chef. Now, I ask you, what's wrong with that?"

"I'm not saying anything's wrong with it," Ogen replied, "all I'm saying is it's a waste." She was not looking at Asaji. Instead, her eyes were lowered as though looking at her hands resting palm-up in her lap, but her gaze was actually fixed on Okaji. "Anyway, I was never given any fish dumplings . . ."

"Giving *you* fish dumplings—now that *really* would have been a waste," shot back Asaji.

"But you make lots of omelet rolls and sweets. If there's always been so much left over, why make such a fuss when the missus started giving me things to take home?"

"Why, you—!" Asaji tried to rise from where he was seated but Shinshichi held onto his arm and restrained him.

Without so much as flinching, Ogen continued. "And you, ma'am

—how about that bowl of tea and rice soup with pickled squid you have there? When you're done slurping the broth, you'll throw the rest away, won't you?"

"Ogen!" Okaji lost her temper. She stared at Ogen, who lowered her eyes to her lap, only to fix them on Okaji again a moment later. "Don't misunderstand me, Ogen. This is a restaurant. People come here to eat. We don't waste food."

"But every day you have food left over."

"What are you talking about?" shouted Okaji, striking the tatami with the palm of her hand. "I can't believe what I'm hearing—I'm going to throw away this rice soup, you say? We have food left over every day, you say? You've got to be kidding! All of this—this rice, Shinshichi's pickled squid—has already been served to our guests and brought in money for this restaurant. I'm not some prima donna who goes around slurping a bit of soup and throwing the rest in the garbage!"

"You should have a look in the garbage out back before you say that, ma'am."

"I've been looking in our garbage for ten years now!" retorted Okaji, raising her voice. "Shinshichi knows how to get the best ingredients—that's his job. And Ohatsu and I know how to get our customers to order what he makes with those ingredients—that's our job. But for whatever reason, on some days, we'll get nothing but old men coming in to eat."

"What's that got to do with it?"

"You can't ask an old man to order something chewy like octopus or squid, now can you? At times like that, no matter how good the ingredients are, we get stuck with leftovers."

"Some customers will order an omelet and then leave without touching it," Shinshichi added bluntly.

"But we never throw it away," said Okaji, picking up where Shinshichi had left off. "Asaji takes everything that's left over—octopus, squid, omelets, eggplants . . . you name it—and he stays up all night concocting all sorts of interesting dishes out of it. We always used to look forward to eating it the next day. But then we started giving all the leftovers to you instead, because you have a big family and I thought you needed the food more than we did. So you see, you've got nothing to complain about."

Without looking entirely convinced, Ogen remained silent. To someone like her who had survived on mud dumplings, Okaji's methods—sneaking around to wholesalers and farmers to buy rice and vegetables when everyone else was going without—must have seemed thoroughly reprehensible.

With great relish, Shinshichi was eating a dish Asaji had made the night before. He had taken fried tofu wrappers and stuffed them with discarded vegetable scraps that he'd chopped up. Then he had simmered them in a heavily seasoned broth of soy sauce and fish stock. Asaji said he thought they'd be perfect for a picnic under the cherry blossoms or the autumn foliage. Shinshichi suggested a few improvements such as asking the tofu shop to make the wrappers a little smaller. Just then, the two men heard Okaji sigh from behind the lattice screen on the other side of the room.

Ogen had not returned to the Moegi since the day of her confrontation with Okaji. Ohatsu had continued at the restaurant as though nothing had happened, but two days earlier she had announced that she wanted to quit.

"It's all your fault, ma'am," she'd said to Okaji. Ohatsu blamed Okaji for the fact that Uhei still had no job and, with Ogen no longer bringing home the Moegi's leftovers, the family had had to go back to eating rice gruel.

Ridiculous! Okaji said to herself. Ohatsu had no grounds for blaming her. Wasn't she the one who'd come to Uhei's rescue when he'd collapsed outside her restaurant's front door? Wasn't she the one who'd given Ogen a job into the bargain? Ohatsu ought to be blaming the salt dealers and the pawnbroker who'd refused to hire Uhei, not her. Not once had Okaji heard Ohatsu speak ill of those other people who had not so much as lifted a finger to help her family.

Despite this, when Okaji heard from Ohatsu that Senta had been beaten up by some longshoremen for trying to muscle in on their work and that now Uhei's parents and his younger son were scavenging for old nails, Okaji could not help regretting that she hadn't found some way to come up with the money Ogen had wanted to borrow.

"It must be because I'm cold-hearted by nature that I got so angry with Ogen," she brooded. She would have like to talk things over with Shinshichi and let him reassure her it wasn't so, but she could never catch him alone without Asaji around.

Okaji did not doubt that her cook had been of aware of her feelings for him for some time. He had even intimated once that he reciprocated them. But it wasn't as though he ever looked at her with a burning passion, or contrived for them to be alone together. Omiyo had made up her mind that it was a case of unrequited love. "It's not that you're not an attractive woman, ma'am—but you *are* two years older than him, after all," she had once said thinking to console Okaji.

Okaji coughed to try to get Shinshichi's attention but he did not turn around. Okaji straightened her collar and stood up from her desk. She decided to go out and collect her bill from one of the Moegi's regular customers and pop over to Yokoamichô in Honjo on the way.

When asked to look after things while Okaji was out, Ohatsu nodded but did not look at her. She had agreed to stay until Okaji could find her replacement. In the meantime she was still sleeping in the smaller of the Moegi's rooms. But according to Omiyo, Ohatsu hadn't gotten a very favorable response from the other restaurant she was hoping to work for. At a time such as this, when there was a surplus of labor and a shortage of jobs, waitresses at restaurants everywhere were choosing to stay put.

Okaji found Omiyo outside the front gate sprinkling water on the ground to keep down the dust. It was now October and the weather had turned cool enough to require a double-layered kimono, but it still hadn't rained more than a handful of times. There were murmurings that this year was shaping up to be another bad year for crops.

Okaji turned down a side street in front of Asakusa Bridge, walking past the Dairokuten Shrine and emerging into Heiemonchô. Then, before crossing Yanagi Bridge, she looked in on the woman who ran the boathouse there.

Hirokôji in Ryôgoku was as crowded as ever. Women trying to

lure customers into an archery range shouted shrilly so as not to be drowned out by a crier at a nearby sideshow hut. Men stood in line waiting their turn outside the street's many barbershops.

But what really attracted Okaji's attention was the crowd of people huddled around a soup kitchen. Thin, emaciated, and covered in sweat and grime, they squatted on the ground slurping bowls of rice porridge, so absorbed in eating that they were completely oblivious to the throngs of passersby and shouts of the criers. To Okaji it was a scene that seemed to belong to some other world.

"I wonder," thought Okaji to herself, "what such people would think of Shinshichi's cooking?" She was sure the starving masses would not pause to appreciate the Moegi's ornate serving dishes. They would gulp down the food and hold the bowl out demanding more. They would not notice the seasonal presentations of autumn leaves and how the cold noodles had been arranged to look like a flowing river. They would laugh at her, saying she was just playing with food.

"Is it playing?" Okaji muttered to herself as she crossed Ryôgoku Bridge. Starving people had no use for cherry blossoms and autumn leaves. To them, even peeling a potato to give it a nice regular shape would have seemed wasteful. No wonder Ogen found it pointless and irritating. Suddenly, Okaji realized she had come to a halt and was staring down at the river. She quickly set off walking again.

In Yokoamichô Okaji had a childhood friend named Oichi, who she loved like a little sister. When they were girls, Oichi was always being teased by smaller children and was quite a crybaby, but at fourteen she became apprenticed to the master printmaker Utagawa Kuniyoshi and had taken the name Yoshihana. Now, at twenty-one, she was more popular an artist than her erstwhile master. This past spring, the Kagaya had released a series of famous views of Edo by her that had proved an enormous success.

When Okaji reached the tobacco shop she turned onto a side street. Oichi's house was the fourth one down on the right, diagonally opposite the tofu shop. The lattice front door made only a slight noise as Okaji slid it open. It seemed to have been recently repaired.

"Who's there?" From beyond the shoji came the sound of a man's voice.

Surprised, Okaji peered at the paper doors, which were brown with age. Oichi lived alone, didn't she? The man opened the shoji and stuck his head out. It was a face Okaji knew well—that of the Kagaya's assistant clerk. He must have come to collect a picture to take to the block carver's.

"Who is it?" This time it was Oichi's voice. It sounded hoarse, as though she were tired.

"It's me!" Okaji stepped into the rather untidy house. Even the dirt floor in the entranceway looked as though it hadn't been swept for some time.

The shop assistant from the Kagaya opened the shoji the rest of the way to reveal Oichi, as Okaji had expected, seated behind a desk in the middle of the dimly lit four-and-half-mat room, picture books and papers scattered about leaving no place left to step.

"What do you call all this?"

"Forgive me. I haven't cleaned for three days." Even as she spoke, Oichi's brush continued to race across the paper in front of her.

The shop assistant began clearing a space for Okaji to sit, pushing some of the books and discarded papers surrounding Oichi into a corner. Before he was finished, Oichi added two or three more strokes to her drawing, put down her brush, and leaned away from her desk.

"Finished!" she announced.

Okaji glanced over at Oichi's desk—an oasis of orderliness amidst a sea of chaos. Laid out on top of it was a drawing on thin Mino paper, its lines of black ink not yet dry. It was a preparatory sketch, showing only the outlines of what would be a finished colored woodblock print. Still, even though the drawing did not contain a great amount of detail, Okaji saw enough to make her frown—it was an erotic print depicting a man and a woman, stark naked, engaged in a lascivious act.

"There's nothing else I can do," said Oichi, noting Okaji's disapproval. "Is there?" she added, looking to the shop assistant for confirmation.

The man nodded, smiling as he rolled Oichi's now dry picture with great care around a tube of old blotting paper. The print was not to be put on sale in the shop but sold at a premium to connoisseurs of erotica, he told Okaji. The Kagaya would make a tidy profit—and

Oichi would receive a substantial commission. "That's just the way the world is these days," he added as he prepared to leave. "Miss Yoshihana's views of Edo are selling very nicely these days, but that's about the only thing that is."

According to the shop assistant, even Oichi's teacher, Kuniyoshi, had taken to drawing erotic prints. The finished products were deluxe affairs, colored and embossed with lots of gold and silver overlay—as a result, Yoshihana and Kuniyoshi put that much more care and effort into their drawings. Yoshihana's prints had quietly amassed a loyal following and were highly sought after, he said as he hurried off. It was clear from his tone that he was not merely trying to flatter Oichi.

"Wait a moment. I'm just about to make some tea," Oichi said to her friend as she rose from her desk. Before doing so, she gathered together the papers strewn around the room and threw them in the wastepaper basket.

Okaji noticed that the kettle sitting on the brazier was already boiling away. Steam rose from beneath the lid, which was slightly askew. The Kagaya's assistant had apparently made himself some tea while waiting for Oichi to finish her sketch.

Oichi picked up the teapot and teacups that were sitting on top of the brazier and went into the kitchen, intending, Okaji presumed, to put fresh tea leaves in the pot. The room fell quiet except for the sound of water boiling in the kettle and, in the background, of teacups being rinsed out in the kitchen.

"Are you in the neighborhood to collect some bills?" asked Oichi from the kitchen.

"That's right," replied Okaji, turning in her direction. "I'm just on my way now."

"That erotic print of mine was pretty good, wasn't it?" Okaji was at a loss for a reply. Along with the sound of running water came Oichi's laughter from the kitchen. "I bet you didn't think I could draw like that."

"Well, no, to be perfectly honest, I didn't."

Oichi appeared again carrying the teapot and cups on a tray. She poured a little of the water she'd brought from the kitchen into the kettle and reached for the tea canister.

"It's like Master Kuniyoshi told me long ago: you can't eat art. He's right—there's a soup kitchen right next to the Kagaya, but none of the people who come there so much as glance at the prints on display out front."

Okaji did not reply. She listened to the sound of hot water being poured into the teapot.

"Fortunately, people are still buying my prints of Edo, but if rice gets any more scarce, the Kagaya won't be able to charge even the pittance they're selling them for now."

"What will you do then, Oichi?" asked Okaji with some hesitation.

"Do?" replied Oichi, looking up at her with a puzzled expression on her face.

"To earn a living."

"Oh, I see . . ."

Okaji nodded as her friend placed a slightly bitter looking cup of tea in front of her.

_____

The next day Kumezô barged into the Moegi during the lunch hour peak.

Okaji was upstairs when she became aware of someone shouting outside in the street. All of a sudden, the sound drew closer, as though whoever it was had come through the front gate. But it wasn't until she heard the voice scream "Okaji!" as it went into her office that she realized it was Kumezô.

Okaji's customers exchanged cautious glances. From downstairs they heard the sound of Shinshichi's voice as he managed to prevent Kumezô from going upstairs, and Kumezô's voice as he tried to push the cook out of his way. Okaji apologized to her customers and stood up.

Scurrying downstairs, she found Ohatsu and Omiyo standing in the corridor in their aprons looking tense and anxious. Okaji tucked the skirt of her kimono into her obi to keep it from trailing on the ground and dashed down the corridor toward her office.

"Get out!" screamed Kumezô. "Okaji, get out!"

As soon as Kumezô saw Okaji he broke free of Shinshichi's grasp and latched onto her. "We have to go! We have to get away!"

"What is it? What's going on?"

Okaji tried to push Kumezô aside but he held fast to her arm. There was a loud sound as the seam of her sleeve ripped apart.

"Let's go that way—out the back!"

"But why? Why do we have to run? Tell me!"

"That loan shark is after me."

"You must be joking."

Still holding onto Okaji, Kumezô leapt down into the kitchen. At the same moment, Okaji pulled her arm away with all her might. There was another loud ripping sound and the sleeve of her kimono came off in Kumezô's hand. Shinshichi caught Okaji as she tumbled backward into her office. Kumezô landed on his hands on the floor of the kitchen.

"Kumezô, you didn't . . ."

"Now is no time to argue."

"You lied and said I was coming back to the Sansuitei so you could borrow more money, didn't you?"

"I had no choice. I was in danger of losing the restaurant."

Kumezô stood up and again tried to grab hold of Okaji. Without fully realizing what she was doing, she slapped him across the face with the palm of her hand.

"I know, it was wrong of me," Kumezô said, pressing his hand to his cheek. "But I don't have time to go into a lengthy apology now—that loan shark and his goons think you deceived them and they're really mad about it."

"That's because *you* deceived them!"

"Look, we don't have time to argue about it." Kumezô tried to pull Okaji into the kitchen but she clung to Shinshichi. Just then, there was a terrible racket from the direction of the front door.

"They're here!" Kumezô screamed, crouching down on the floor of the kitchen. The loan shark's henchmen had kicked down the front door.

"Okaji! You lied to us," shouted one of the men as he came running down the corridor in his sandals. "You and that no-good husband of yours!"

"You said you were going to use it to remodel the Sansuitei," chimed in another. "Do you take us for fools? How're you gonna remodel it when the place is mortgaged two or three times over?"

"I didn't know anything about—"

"Shut up! Don't play dumb," yelled a third man.

The first man kicked over the lattice screen in Okaji's office. It was a signal to the others to begin their rampage. The second man swept the saké pots and all the good dishware off the shelf behind Okaji. The third leapt into the kitchen and threw everything he could lay his hands on—fish, eggs, a basket full of uncooked rice—out the back door. From the direction of the front of the restaurant came the sound of dishes breaking as one or two of their confederates ransacked the dining room.

"Shinshichi. Go look after the customers."

Shinshichi nodded and left the office. Okaji went and sat in a corner. At some point, Kumezô had vanished. In the kitchen, Asaji and Shôkichi stood motionless over by the oven. Okaji heard the sound of sobbing from out in the hall. Instead of leaving Okaji and the customers to their fate and fleeing, Ohatsu and Omiyo, now in tears, still stood at the bottom of the stairs.

The ruffians rolled up their sleeves and began rampaging through the rest of the restaurant. Shoji were pulled off their runners and stomped to pieces. Fusuma doors were tossed into the street.

Okaji watched it all impassively. She knew the men's violence was calculated—if they did too much damage they'd never get their money back, so they just wanted to make a lot of noise. One of them picked up a saké pot that hadn't broken the first time and smashed it on the kitchen floor. Another kicked the lattice screen lying on the floor for good measure.

Just then, outside in the street Okaji heard someone shout something about a riot.

"Come quickly, everyone! It's a riot!"

"No, you're wrong—it's not a riot!" protested Okaji, turning pale and standing up. The loan shark's thugs immediately stopped what they were doing, but this did nothing to quell the commotion outside in the street, which continued until the restaurant had been emptied of its customers.

Okaji ran to the front door. One of the loan shark's men threw a teacup at her, hitting her on the shoulder, but she felt no pain at all. She leaped from the hallway onto the dirt floor where the lattice door still lay just as the men had left it, and ran outside into the garden in her stocking feet. A large crowd of people had already assembled outside the front gate. It seemed they had been waiting in line for their free ration of government rice at a nearby rice shop.

From inside the Moegi came the sound of a dish shattering.

"Riot!"

It was impossible to tell from where the shout had come. A strange cry arose from the mob and people began pushing past one another to get through the gate.

"Stop!" Okaji cried. She was sent flying into the bushes as she tried to block their way. People poured past her and through the front door of the Moegi. Some tripped on the lattice door and fell down, to be trampled by those behind them. There were screams and shouts. As the chaos spread through the restaurant the loan shark's men came rushing out.

Okaji floundered about in the shrubbery, the clipped, rounded branches of a boxwood hedge poking into her. By the time she managed to free herself, her face, arms, and legs covered in scratches, a steady stream of people drawn by the commotion were pouring into the Moegi.

The situation was now completely out of control. People began filing out of the Moegi after partaking in the plunder. Okaji sobbed hysterically as she watched her possessions go by. One man lugged away her rice chest, another went off cradling her strongbox. Women clutched kimonos, others her smoking set and mirror stand. To Okaji they all looked like Uhei and Ogen.

"But I didn't do anything!" wailed Okaji, pounding the ground with her fists. But no one so much as turned to look at her.

The last ones to leave were a man carting away a kettle for cooking rice and a woman making off with a soup pot. Then the Moegi fell quiet. The nearby shops must have all lowered their shutters during the commotion, for when the footsteps of these last two died away there was not a single person left in the street.

"This is the end of the Moegi," Okaji thought to herself. She was sure the looters had made off with every scrap of food, every piece of furniture, every shred of clothing she had, without leaving so much as a single hand towel behind.

There was no sign the looters had attacked any of the other shops on the street. Far from feeling sympathy for Okaji, the neighboring merchants were no doubt breathing a sigh of relief that the mob's fury had subsided without the destruction spreading to their businesses as well.

Okaji lay face down on the ground. Her tears soaked into the hard, dry soil. All of a sudden she sensed that someone was standing nearby. Lifting her head slightly, she saw a pair of sturdy, leather-soled sandals. They belonged to Shinshichi.

"The customers are all safe," he said, kneeling down and helping Okaji sit up.

Okaji said nothing. She had forgotten she had asked Shinshichi to get the customers out of the restaurant—forgotten that there *were* even any customers, in fact.

"Just look at it, Shinshichi! Look at it," she repeated, shutting her eyes and burying her face in Shinshichi's chest. "It's a mess." She was unable to hear Shinshichi's answer. "After all that—leaving the Sansuitei, opening the Moegi, finding you . . . it was all starting to bear fruit."

"But you don't mean you're giving up now?"

"This is the end. I've had enough. Why can't a woman run her own restaurant just because food is scarce?"

"That's why . . ." Shinshichi hesitatingly drew Okaji toward him. "You have to rebuild the Moegi."

"No, I can't."

"You must." Okaji pulled away from Shinshichi and looked at him, but he shyly looked away and embraced her more tightly. He did not let go. "What is it they say? Even if you prune all the branches off a tree leaving just the trunk, new branches will start to bud . . ."

"But I'm penniless. There's no trunk left for a bud to grow on."

"It's only a little, but I have some money my sister's looking after for me."

"But that's money you've saved up to start your own restaurant someday, right?"

"Why do you think I'm still a bachelor at my age? It's because . . ." Shinshichi's voice trailed off without finishing his sentence. Okaji wanted to know what he was going to say but Shinshichi let go of her and stood up.

Asaji and Shôkichi were walking toward them. Then Ohatsu and Omiyo emerged from the back door of the restaurant. "We'd better start cleaning up right away," said Asaji, "or we won't be able to reopen." Apparently, no one else seemed to think that the Moegi was finished.

Suddenly Okaji felt a shadow fall over her. She looked up. Standing there with a bruise under one eye was Ogen, holding a strongbox— Okaji's strongbox—the same one she had seen a man making off with a moment earlier.

"We got it back for you—my son and I did." Ogen's shoulders heaved up and down as she spoke, evidently worked up from her exertions. She must have received the black eye in the process.

"You'll be needing this, won't you?" she said. "The food you make here is expensive, after all." Ogen put the strongbox on the ground in front of Okaji. Then, licking her finger and rubbing saliva on her bruise, she turned to go. She hadn't even asked whether Okaji was hurt or tried to comfort her by telling her not to lose hope.

"Wait!" Okaji tried to get up and go after Ogen but she felt a sharp pain in her ankle as though she had sprained it. Ohatsu held out a hand and helped Okaji up. As she rose, Okaji looked down at the strongbox at her feet.

Okaji's tree had once been covered with lush foliage. The leaves had fallen, but they had grown back more lushly than before. Now, its trunk had been stripped bare of branches, but new ones would soon start to bud out all over again.

SELECTED DALKEY ARCHIVE PAPERBACKS

SELECTED DALKEY ARCHIVE PAPERBACKS

FOR A FULL LIST OF PUBLICATIONS, VISIT:
www.dalkeyarchive.com